Darcy's Favorite

By Zoe Burton

Darcy's Favorite

Zoe Burton

Published by Zoe Burton

Drafts of this story were written and posted on fan fiction forums in July and August 2021.

ISBN-13: 978-1-953138-12-5

Acknowledgements

First, I thank Jesus Christ, my Savior and Guide. Without you, I could not have written this story. I love you!

Additional thanks go to my friends, Rose and Leenie, for their support and unconditional love.

My Patreon patrons also deserve a great big Thank You, as well, for their patience and support.

Table of Contents

Chapter 1

Elizabeth Bennet settled into the window seat in her bedchamber, correspondence in hand. Her elder sister, Jane, was currently in London visiting their aunt, uncle, and cousins, but had taken the time to write Elizabeth a good, long letter. Eagerly, she broke the seal, unfolded the missive, and began to read.

> *Gracechurch Street, London*
>
> *21 February, 1809*
>
> *Dearest Lizzy,*
>
> *I have such wonderful news! I think I may have met the man of my dreams. His name is Mr. Charles Bingley, and he is the son of a textile merchant from the North of England.*
>
> *I can hear you now, Sister, and I know that you are asking me how I met Mr. Bingley. I will tell you … Aunt and Uncle Gardiner attended a ball just a few days after I arrived for my visit, and they took me with them. There, making his way around the room, was the most gloriously beautiful gentleman I had ever seen. He is tall and athletic, with reddish-blonde hair and green eyes. He is the most amiable young man I have ever met!*

Immediately upon making our acquaintance, Mr. Bingley asked me to dance. We fell into quite an easy conversation during our set. No awkward silences there! Afterward, he remained by my side for most of the evening, though he did do his duty and dance with other ladies, as I did with other gentlemen.

Mr. Bingley requested permission to call on me that night, and has done so every day for the last fortnight! How wonderful it is to have such a handsome and friendly gentleman sit in the parlor across from me. We have discovered that our tastes are similar, and our dispositions appear to be the same. He is perfect!

I was also introduced to Mr. Bingley's father and younger sister. Miss Bingley was everything a well-bred lady should be, and I hope she and I may become friends. The elder Mr. Bingley, Mr. Augustus Bingley, is a long-time friend of Uncle's. I have never met him before because I usually come at the beginning of the season and the Bingleys come in March, when I am on my way home. We seem to have just missed each other the last year or two.

Upon meeting Mr. Augustus Bingley, I could immediately see where

Mr. Charles Bingley got his good looks, for the father is every bit as handsome as the son. Should we marry, I need never fear waking one day to an ugly man.

Oh, Lizzy, how I wish you were here to meet him, and to share in my joy! I have written to Father to ask to extend my stay a few weeks, to give me the opportunity to get to know Mr. Charles Bingley better.

I will write more as soon as I can. I am eager to see you in person, to give you all the little details that were too time consuming to relate in writing.

Your loving sister,

Jane

Elizabeth squealed with joy as she read her most beloved sibling's words. She jumped up, running to the desk and pulling out paper, quill, and ink. Then, she sat and wrote a heartfelt reply.

~~~***~~~

Fitzwilliam Darcy accepted the post from the housekeeper, dismissing her as he began to sort the envelopes into piles. Near the bottom of the stack, his hand hovered over a blotch-covered missive.

Zoe Burton

"Bingley," he said to himself, head shaking. "How you get anything accomplished via correspondence is beyond me." Darcy set his friend's note to the side and finished separating the rest of the letters. Then, he poured himself a cup of tea from the service the housekeeper had delivered with the post, and picked Bingley's note up again. He broke the seal, unfolded the page, and then spent a few moments squinting at it, trying to decipher the other man's terrible handwriting.

Scarborough, Yorkshire

15 July, 1810

Dear Darcy,

My year of mourning for my father is finally over and I feel free again! There is still a hole in my heart where Papa used to be, but I fear that will never leave me. However, a year of no entertainment is arduous for someone who enjoys society as much as I do. I know my father would be happy for me being able to attend soirees again.

As you know, I have been looking for an estate to let near the home of my betrothed. My solicitor has finally located one. It is called Netherfield Park and is a mere three miles from Miss Bennet's home. I hope you will acquit me of sounding needy or grasping, but I wish to remind you of your promise to be my best man, and to help me settle into the estate. We will not take possession until Michaelmas, so you have time to take care of anything you must before you join me in Hertfordshire.

As for Miss Bennet, I know you were concerned about our engagement, especially given the fact that she and I have not seen each other in a twelve-month. Let me reassure you by telling you that she is an absolute angel and I am quite happy to fulfill the contract Father made for me to wed her. We were granted permission to write to each other this past year, and have done so faithfully. Miss Jane Bennet is as beautiful inside as I recall her being on the outside. I have every faith that she shares my feelings of joy at the thought of being married to each other.

I look forward to meeting you in town in mid-September. You can ride with us, if you wish, or take your own equipage, if that is your preference.

Yours,

C. Bingley

Darcy leaned back, dropping the hand holding the letter to the arm of his chair. *Hmmm,* he thought, cocking his head to listen in vain for the sounds of the pianoforte. He glanced out the window of his study, watching the neighbors promenade up and down the street on their way to the entrance to Hyde Park. He sighed. *I know Georgiana has suffered a horrible experience, but she seems to be recovering so slowly. I miss hearing her notes as she practices the pianoforte and I miss her giggles as she chats with her friends.* He chewed his lip. *Will she be well if I visit my friend as scheduled? Drat that Wickham, anyway!*

For several moments, Darcy relived the frightening events of the spring. His only sister, a dozen years younger than he, was kidnapped from Hyde Park. His late father's godson, George Wickham, in collusion with Georgiana's governess, Mrs. Younge, and two other dissolute and disreputable persons, had planned out the seizure of the fourteen-year-old.

Thankfully for Darcy, he was not the only guardian his sister had, and the other, his cousin, Colonel Richard Fitzwilliam, had connections to excellent covert investigators. The moment he had received the ransom note, he had called for Fitzwilliam, and within four and twenty hours, Georgiana was home, safe and sound, though emotionally overwrought.

Mrs. Younge disappeared, Darcy speculated into the teeming streets of one of the poorer sections of London. Wickham had come to him, begging for a ticket on a ship to Canada or America. Fitzwilliam had promised to kill him if he caught him. Wickham had long been terrified of the other man, and now that the colonel had seen action on the continent, was even more so. Darcy revenged his sister for a full quarter hour, taking his own pound of flesh out of his former friend, before agreeing to the purchase. Months later, he presumed Wickham was on the far side of the ocean. Of the other conspirators, one was dead at the hands of an unknown assailant. Fitzwilliam's investigator friends were still tracking down the other.

Darcy unconsciously crumpled Bingley's letter when he clenched his fists. Rage at the thought of the kidnapper remaining unpunished threatened to overwhelm him. He closed his eyes and breathed deeply, exhaling slowly as he fought to push the feelings down. When he calmed, he smoothed out the crinkled letter on the top of his desk. "Aunt Audra says I should keep my appointment with my friend, and that time will heal Georgiana's pain. I hope she is correct."

Sighing to himself, Darcy pulled out a sheet of paper, sharpened a quill, and dipped the tip in ink. He first wrote a note to his friend, confirming his attendance upon him in Hertfordshire, then made a list of things that must be accomplished before he joined Bingley.

Chapter 2

Hertfordshire

September 28, 1810

Darcy followed Bingley into the well-maintained house at Longbourn estate. The gentlemen, along with Bingley's sisters and brother-in-law, had arrived in the area just two hours earlier. Bingley had not wanted to wait longer to visit the home of his betrothed, and had prevailed upon Darcy to accompany him, since his family would not.

"Mr. Charles Bingley and Mr. Fitzwilliam Darcy." The housekeeper, Mrs. Hill, stepped to the side to allow the gentlemen to enter, then curtsied and backed out of the room, pulling the door shut behind her.

Darcy bowed alongside his friend and then listened as Bingley greeted one of the young ladies.

"Miss Bennet! How good it is to see you. Thank you for your letters." Bingley grasped Jane's hand and did not let go, smiling at her light blush.

"I am happy you enjoyed them. Thank you for your replies." Jane's serene smile was contrasted with the shine in her eyes.

"I could not let such delightful missives go unanswered." Bingley glanced around. "Will you introduce me to your family?"

"Oh! Yes, I will." Jane turned slightly, as much as she could with one hand firmly clasped by her betrothed, and indicated her mother and sisters with her free hand. "This is my mother, Mrs. Thomas Bennet, and these are my sisters, Elizabeth, Mary, Kitty, and Lydia."

Bingley smiled at each lady and bowed. "I am happy to meet you all. Please allow me to introduce my friend to you. This is Mr. Fitzwilliam Darcy of London and Pemberley in Derbyshire."

Darcy bowed again. This time, when he stood up, one of Miss Jane Bennet's sisters caught his eye and attention. *What was her name?* His mind scrambled to recall. *Elizabeth? Yes! That is what it was ... Elizabeth.* When she smiled at him, he lifted his lips in a quick answering smile but immediately turned his gaze away. However, though he was facing another sister, his entire focus was on Elizabeth. His heart pounded as though he had just completed a foot race. He swallowed and willed himself to calm down.

"Welcome to Longbourn, sir." Mrs. Bennet and her daughters curtseyed again. "We are delighted to have you here. Please be seated." She gestured toward the furniture arranged in the center of the room.

Thanking their hostess, Darcy and Bingley chose seats. Bingley settled onto a sofa next to Jane. Darcy took a single step toward the couple, thinking to sit on the other side of his friend, but one of the younger girls took the spot. Looking around, he saw that the only place open was next to Elizabeth.

"You must sit beside Lizzy, Mr. Darcy." Mrs. Bennet urged him to sit next to her second daughter. "My husband is in a wheeled chair; he and I will sit at the table with Kitty and Lydia." She gestured toward a table arranged at the end of the seating area and near one of the tall windows.

With a dip of his head, Darcy acquiesced, sitting gingerly beside the young lady who had so captured his attention a moment ago. When Elizabeth smiled at him, Darcy gave her a brief one of his own in return, but for a reason he could not fathom, being this close to her scrambled his senses. He could think of nothing to say. His heart pounded so hard he was certain she could hear it, and he felt a trickle of sweat run down his back under his fine shirt. He swallowed and cast another glance her way. He both avoided looking at her and could not help staring.

Before Darcy was even settled into his seat, he was required to rise again, for the door opened and an older gentleman about the age his own father would have been, had he lived, was pushed into the room by a male servant. Miss Bennet took it upon herself to introduce her father to the visitors.

"I am pleased to make your acquaintance." Mr. Bennet made a half-bow from his chair. "Forgive me for not standing. My heart is weak and I must remain still, lest it become overexcited and stop beating." When his wife let out a cry, the older gentleman chuckled before speaking to her. "There, there, Mrs. Bennet. I am well. There is no need to take on so. One of your daughters is betrothed and soon to marry; you should be rejoicing."

Darcy's brow creased as he witnessed the Bennet patriarch tease his wife. He did not know what to make of it. He was unused to seeing gentlemen make sport of their spouses to their faces. He did not know what to say, and so remained silent.

"Feel free to resume your seats." Mr. Bennet gestured to the servant to push him closer to the table, then dismissed him.

"Papa." The youngest daughter spoke in a loud voice that drew the attention of everyone in the room. "I saw the prettiest ribbon at the milliner's, but I have spent my allowance. Mary still has some of hers but will not share with me. Make her buy me the ribbon, please?"

"No, Lydia, I will not. Mary's funds are hers to do with as she pleases. If she does not wish to get you a ribbon, she does not have to."

"But, Papa, she-!"

"Enough!" Mr. Bennet's harsh word stopped his daughter's oncoming tirade but sparked his wife's anxiety.

"Lydia! Do not aggravate your father so!" Mrs. Bennet's hands twisted her handkerchief into a rope. "If he dies, we will be thrown into the hedgerows by that awful Mr. Collins!"

The housekeeper entered at that moment, distracting the matron. Darcy took a deep breath in the relative quiet that followed the servant's arrival. He glanced at Elizabeth and was struck again by her fine eyes. When she turned them in his direction, a perplexed look creasing her brow, his heart picked up its pace again. Struck once more by the unfamiliar stirrings, he looked away.

When Mrs. Bennet finally handed him a cup of tea a few minutes later, his hand shook. Darcy quickly lowered the delicate porcelain to rest on his knee. Elizabeth sat quietly at his side. Though she made one or two brief attempts to draw him out, when he remained silent, she apparently gave up the notion and turned her attention to her sister and Bingley.

Eventually, the misery ended, and Bingley rose to leave.

"You must stay for dinner!" Mrs. Bennet's exclamation sounded almost desperate.

"I would love to, but I promised my sisters I would be back to eat with them. I give you my word I will stay another day and dine with you all." Bingley's jovial reply appeased the matron and within a few moments, they were ascending into the carriage for the ride back to Netherfield.

"Well, Darcy, what do you think?" Bingley beamed at his friend from across the equipage.

"About what?" Darcy remained unsettled, and so did not catch Bingley's meaning.

Bingley leaned forward. "About Miss Bennet!"

Darcy felt stupid for not realizing what his friend would be asking about. "She seems like a perfectly lovely young woman."

"She is. I told you, she is perfect." Bingley sat back, crossing his arms.

"Well, I do not know about that. No one is perfect. However, she did seem to ..." Darcy trailed off as he tried to recall the eldest Bennet's looks and behavior as she interacted with the other gentleman.

"Yes?" Bingley was leaning forward again, eyebrows quirked over glowing green irises.

"She seemed to light up when we entered, I noticed. She was very proper." Darcy hesitated. "She smiles too much."

"Smiles too much." Bingley rolled his eyes. "I do not know where you get these ideas. She seemed pleased to see me, I thought. Do you agree?"

"I do. She paid little attention to anyone else, though that could just mean she wished to garner your favor."

"Since we are betrothed and she is to be my wife, she undoubtedly does." Bingley shook his head. "I know Caroline has probably entreated you to persuade me to break the engagement. Do you agree with her?"

Darcy shook his head. "Frankly, no. You are honor-bound to marry her. If you broke the engagement, the family could sue. You do not want that. I explained this to your sister. She did not appear to hear me, however."

"Caroline only hears what she wishes to." Bingley was silent for a moment. He looked down and played with a corner of his coat. "Do you think Miss Bennet might care for me? I find myself feeling rather fond of her, you see." He looked up. "I would much rather she feels the same."

Darcy shrugged. "I cannot read her mind, so I really have no idea. However, her behavior indicates she might."

Bingley was quiet for a moment as he considered his friend's words. "Well, then, I have a few weeks to *make* her fall in love with me. I should get to it."

Darcy chuckled. "Indeed, you should. If anyone can make a lady fall in love with him, it is you."

The remainder of the trip was spent in silence. The conversation had left Bingley with much to consider, and Darcy with his equilibrium returned.

~~~***~~~

At Longbourn, the Bennet ladies remained in the drawing room long after the gentlemen had excused themselves. They exclaimed over Bingley and his attention to Jane, and over Darcy and his reserve.

"He stared at Lizzy quite a bit," Lydia declared.

"He did not." Elizabeth instantly refuted her youngest sister's words. "He barely looked at me at all, and spoke even less."

"Oh, but he did, Lizzy!" Kitty defended Lydia's statement. "Every time I looked your direction, he had his eyes on you."

Elizabeth just shook her head, refusing to argue over it. Eventually, after more pushing on the subject from her sisters, she began to feel irrationally irritated. She stood. "I am going for a walk. I will return in time to dine, Mama." She headed for the doorway.

"Be back before that; you will need to change your gown before you eat." Mrs. Bennet waved her handkerchief. "Why a beautiful and clever child like you must be such a trial to my nerves I will never understand."

Elizabeth smirked as she listened to her mother fuss, but continued out the front door and into the woods to her favorite path.

As she strode away, she remembered the frown on their guest's face whenever Kitty and Lydia giggled and carried on.

"If Mr. Darcy stared at me, it was only to find fault," she said to herself. "It was clear he did not like any of us." She shrugged. "Though how he could make such a judgement on so little as an introduction is the question." Picking up a long, thin branch that had fallen off one of the trees in a recent storm, she began to swish the underbrush that grew alongside her path. Eventually, she reached the trail to her favorite spot, Oakham Mount. She hesitated for a moment, conscious of the time, but in the end, decided her need for mental clarity was more important than her mother's need for her to look her best.

The path up the hill was not a particularly arduous one. Oakham Mount was not really a mountain; instead it was more of a high spot. However, it afforded an excellent view of Longbourn and the surrounding tenant farms, and Elizabeth loved to sit at the top and watch her home and all the activity in and around it. Vowing to herself not to tarry too long, she did not settle comfortably on top of the boulder that marked the peak. Instead, she leaned against it and allowed her mind to ponder their recent guests.

"He is so handsome, Mr. Darcy is." Elizabeth sighed as she spoke out loud. "I would have liked to get to know him better, but what is the use? He clearly disapproved of Lydia's behavior, especially." She fell silent for a long moment, allowing herself to feel the disappointment. "I could not marry someone who did not like my family, so I suppose it is best I discover this now." She straightened. "I will guard my heart, then. Perhaps I will not need to be in his company often." With a shrug, she turned to make her way down the hill and back to the house.

Chapter 3

True to his word, Bingley returned the next day, as soon as it was polite to visit. With him, in addition to Darcy, he brought his older sister and her husband, Louisa and Reginald Hurst, and his younger sister, Caroline.

As Darcy waited out the new round of introductions, his gaze wandered the room, examining each member of the Bennet family. Without realizing it, his eyes landed on Elizabeth, remaining for several minutes. *Her features are irregular,* he thought. *When she is quiet, as she is now, there is nothing remarkable about her. It is those eyes, and the manner in which her entire face lights up when she- ... there it is!* All thought – and his breath – ceased as the object of his attention smiled at his friends. When she turned and strolled to the other side of the room, he noted her light and pleasing figure. He swallowed. *What is it about her that draws me so?* He was startled out of his contemplation when Bingley nudged him and tipped his head toward the seating area.

Looking around, Darcy noted Bingley's sisters seating themselves together on a sofa. Hurst joined them, filling the one empty space. There was a chair nearby that was empty, and a seat beside Bingley and Jane.

Elizabeth, he noted, was sitting down next to her younger sisters at the table. With a mental shrug, he chose the chair near Hurst and settled in.

Mrs. Bennet fluttered around, much as she had the previous day, chattering to her guests. The tea service was brought in and she set to pouring. The youngest girls sat as they had the day before, at the table near the window. Darcy could not see what they were doing, but whatever it was seemed to require much in the way of giggles and whispers. Suddenly, they jumped up and ran across the room. He waited for their mother to rebuke their behavior, but she did not. His brow creased.

They are unchecked, Darcy thought. *It seems to me that it might be a regular occurrence. That is not good; when they are older, it could lead to trouble. But, I am not their father, and the household is probably feeling a strain due to Mr. Bennet's condition.* Darcy felt compelled, having identified a problem, to alleviate or correct it. The problem was, he was a stranger to the girls and wholly unconnected; he knew they would not look at him as an authority figure. *However, they may be willing to see me as an elder brother.* Darcy felt a spark of hope light in his chest. How to approach them became his next concern.

As Darcy fell deep in contemplation of the problem he had set himself to, he was unaware that he had ceased to pay attention to the rest of the room's occupants, or that two of the ladies were engaged in observing his behavior. His unseeing gaze was often on the floor in front of his feet, but was just as frequently trained upon Elizabeth.

To Elizabeth, it seemed as though Darcy truly did dislike her young sisters. She again felt an arrow of disappointment, because he was the most handsome gentleman she had ever met, and he had a pleasingly deep voice that washed over her like a soothing cup of chocolate. She pulled her gaze away from him, biting her lip. She looked down for a moment, but then felt her courage rise. She lifted her chin and turned her attention to her mother, who was relating with great energy a tale about Jane that was meant to paint the older girl in a flattering light. She continued to ignore Darcy for the remainder of his visit.

To Caroline Bingley, it seemed that Darcy found the Bennet family unsuitable, and she was almost gleeful about it. She lifted her chin, looking down her nose as the youngest girls raced past her. However, what she saw next had her narrowing her eyes. Darcy appeared to be staring at Elizabeth, and Caroline did not like it one bit. *Surely, he cannot be attracted to her,* she thought. *There is not one good feature in her face. She appears to lack any fashion sense; why, she is practically dowdy! What can be the fascina-*

tion? I must do something about this. Her attention was required to reply to a question from her hostess, but in the back of Caroline's mind, she was working out a strategy to diminish Elizabeth's appeal to Darcy.

A short time later, her ruminations were interrupted again, this time by her brother.

"We have no engagements this evening; we would be happy to remain to dine with you. Would we not, Caroline?" Bingley's eager smile told his sister that he desired to spend more time with his betrothed and her family.

Caroline paused before answering. She did not wish to spend any more time than she had to with this family, but she could not insist they return to Netherfield without looking churlish. With an internal sigh, she smiled. "We would be delighted." She gritted her teeth when Mrs. Bennet clapped happily, accompanying the action with a loud exclamation.

Jane thanked her soon-to-be sisters for their consideration. "You have been here all afternoon already. Perhaps you would like to freshen up a bit? We have plenty of space in the guest wing of the house; it would be no trouble for the maid to carry up some water for washing. You could even lie down and rest, if you wish. Sally is an excellent dresser."

Caroline hesitated, uncertain she wished to leave Bingley alone with this family for very long, even if he was marrying into it.

The matter was decided, however, when Louisa swiftly accepted.

"That would be lovely, Miss Bennet. I confess a nap would do me a world of good. I did not sleep well last night; I never do in a new place. It always takes several days before I become accustomed to the particular sounds of a house." Louisa clasped her hands in her lap, leaning forward with an earnest smile.

Caroline did her best to hide the roll of her eyes. *Louisa is far too much like Charles,* she thought, *too eager to be happy and pleased.* She sniffed. She again gave in graciously, not wishing to make a bad impression. "Indeed; a rest would be delightful."

Jane rang the bell, informing the housekeeper of what she needed, and within a few minutes, Caroline and Louisa were ascending the stairs ahead of Mrs. Hill.

~~~***~~~

Back in the drawing room, Darcy had been pulled away from his contemplations by a similar offer. He and Bingley withdrew to the guest chambers whose use had been extended to them.

In his borrowed room, Darcy used the water to wash his face and hands. Then, he allowed the footman to assist him out of his tailcoat and boots and reclined on the bed.

Lifting his arms and tucking his hands under his head, he permitted himself to relax as his mind wandered.

I still have not thought of a way to approach the youngest girls. I think I need to get to know them better. Perhaps I may engage them in conversation as the opportunity arises. I cannot behave as their parent. Darcy nodded to himself, satisfied with this plan of action. He closed his eyes as his thoughts moved from the youngest sisters to the second eldest. He sighed as his heart clenched at the thought of going back to London and never seeing her again.

What is wrong with me? I never react to ladies in such a manner. His mind wandered to a place where he proposed and Elizabeth accepted, then on to a new scene, where he introduced her to the earl and countess, as well as his few Darcy relatives. He imagined their reactions, which he did not think would be positive and welcoming. His eyes popped open. The peace and joy he felt at his hypothetical engagement disintegrated into fear, anger, and frustration. In his mind, he could see her crying as they slighted her and her upbringing, and, in some future time, resenting him and her situation. He leaped off the bed and paced across the room to the window, where he leaned against the frame and looked out. *I cannot do it.* A feeling of loneliness came over him like a wave on the seashore, a sensation he had experienced more and more frequently of late. Feeling as though he could burst into tears, he pushed away from the window frame and threw himself upon the bed. *It does not matter how I feel. I would not subject any woman to such things. I cannot have her and that is that.*

At dinner, despite his admonishment to himself, Darcy found that he could not force himself away from Elizabeth. She drew him like a bee to a flower, and he was powerless to ignore her. Strangely, try as he might, he could not get close to her. It was almost as if she were avoiding him. *It is impossible,* he told himself. *Why would she avoid me?*

~~~***~~~

At the end of the evening, as the Netherfield party rode home in Darcy's carriage, Caroline began to wax eloquent on the inferiority of the Bennets. Darcy listened in silence to her tirade.

"None of them will ever be accepted in polite society, you know. The youngest girls are wild, the mother is almost as bad, and the father only laughs, when he is present at all."

Bingley immediately protested. "Mr. Bennet is ill, Caroline. That would cause any family to feel a strain, and induce behavior that may not be the usual. Surely you recall how you felt those few hours between when Father fell ill and when he passed? Imagine that uncertainty dragging on for months or years!"

"Oh, I am quite certain this behavior has been going on far longer than the length of Mr. Bennet's indisposition." Caroline sniffed and lifted her chin. "Even without that, the family is unsuitable. Judging from the look of the place, those girls have little in the way of a dowry. Father should have chosen higher for you. You are his heir, after all."

"If that is a hint for me to disclose to you the amount of Jane's portion, I will tell you now I am ignoring it. The contents of her settlement are private and will remain that way." Bingley crossed his arms and sat back. "If I have told you once, I have told you a dozen times, Jane is the daughter of a gentleman. A connection with her and her family will raise our consequence simply because Mr. Bennet is a landowner. Not that we need the connection; once I purchase an estate, I will be a landowner, as well." When Caroline tried to speak over him, Bingley simply raised his voice and kept talking. "Jane and I are well-suited and we like each other very much. Father wanted me to be happy above all, and I *am* happy with my Jane. Very much so. I should hope you would want the same."

"There is no reason you cannot be happy with someone of higher status than Jane Bennet. We are trying to rise up from trade, not be dragged back down into it." Caroline's tone of voice became sharp.

"I will not jilt Jane and that is the end of it." Bingley suddenly flared into anger, his voice rising. "I am in love with her and she shares my feelings. I would marry her if she had nothing."

Tired of the bickering, Darcy added his two pence to the conversation. "As I have told you several times before, he cannot break the engagement. The Bennets could, and likely would, sue him. He would be required to pay for representation, and then pay reparations to Miss Bennet and the family. Not only would your brother's coffers be reduced significantly, his reputation would be damaged, as would yours, Miss Bingley. Do you truly wish to find yourself marrying whoever would have you because you could find no better?"

Caroline began to sputter, but Darcy tuned her out. He looked out the carriage window as the vehicle rolled up Netherfield's drive. *She is correct, you know,* he thought. *The Bennets would never be accepted.* He sighed to himself, heart heavy.

Chapter 4

Immediately upon returning to Netherfield, Bingley and his family adjourned to the family parlor. Darcy excused himself.

"It has been a long day and I am weary. Would it offend you if I retired for the night?"

"Of course not! This is your home as long as you are here." Bingley clapped a hand on Darcy's shoulder. "You are to feel free to do as you wish. I confess, I do not foresee myself staying down here very long. Caroline has pushed me to the edges of my temper. I plan to have one drink and then head to bed myself."

"I will say good night, then. Are we shooting in the morning?" Darcy stepped toward the staircase.

"We are. Hurst wished to be out early, so make sure you are up at dawn if you want to join us."

Darcy snorted to himself. "When has that ever been a problem?" He grinned when his friend laughed, and with a wave, began to ascend the staircase.

Once in his suite of rooms, he dropped into a chair in front of the fireplace, where a warm blaze danced.

"Would you care for a drop of port, sir?" Mr. Smith, Darcy's valet, appeared at his elbow with a carafe and a glass.

"I would, thank you." Darcy accepted the tumbler full of red liquid. "Give me a quarter hour to enjoy this and I will be along."

Smith bowed and returned to the dressing room, leaving the carafe on the table at his employer's elbow.

Darcy took a generous sip of the wine, then rested the glass, held firmly in his hand, on the arm of the wingback chair. He leaned his head back and thought over the events at dinner. He smiled at the surprised delight he had seen in the middle Bennet girl's eyes when he complimented her technical skill on the pianoforte. "Miss Kitty and Miss Lydia were astonished, I think, to hear me speak so, especially given the terribly dirge-like song their sister was playing," he murmured to himself. "But, it did open a path to communication between us. Hopefully, I can do some good there. I would hate for any young lady to suffer what Georgiana did while I sat by and did nothing."

As they had before, Darcy's ponderings brought Elizabeth to his mind's eye. He recalled the thud of his heart when she turned her fine eyes in his direction. He felt again the racing of his blood in his veins when he drew near to her, and the confusion when she refused to engage him in more than superficial conversation and moved away from him.

I do not know why you are so worried about her avoiding you. You have decided you cannot have her. She does not fit the description your family has given you of a proper wife. Darcy lifted the glass and stared into it, biting his lip. With a shrug and a sigh, he tossed back what remained and set the glass on the table. Then, he rose and headed into the dressing room to prepare for bed.

~~~***~~~

The following days were busy ones for Darcy and the gentlemen of Netherfield. After a successful morning of shooting, during which they caught a number of birds to present to the cook for supper, they went to their rooms to change clothes, then met the ladies in the entry hall. The group was headed to Longbourn's church this morning, at Bingley's insistence.

The Netherfield party arrived in good time, Bingley having ordered the coachman to not spare the whip. Mr. Rossiter followed his instructions to the letter, to the dismay of the ladies, whose exclamations filled the interior, making the gentlemen chuckle or frown, or both, depending upon their nature. Soon, the group was making their way into the small but beautiful building.

"Jane! Mr. Bingley is here!" Lydia Bennet's loud whisper carried all the way to the door from the front.

Jane blushed and stopped her forward motion into the family's pew. She looked toward the back of the church to see her betrothed striding forward, nearly dragging his younger sister along beside him.

"Miss Bennet, good morning." Bingley bowed to his future wife. "I thought perhaps I could sit with you this morning."

"You may." Jane's countenance lit with pleasure, though her smile remained its usual serene lift of the lips.

Darcy observed all of this from over Louisa's shoulder as he walked behind her. It was difficult to miss the pleasure on Jane's face at seeing Bingley this morning, which cemented his friend's happiness in his mind. When the group was again reunited, he suggested the rest of the party sit in the pew behind the Bennets, a scheme quickly agreed upon. Darcy entered first, moving sideways along the narrow space.

When he came to the middle of the row, Darcy took pains to acknowledge each of the other Bennet ladies, beginning with Elizabeth. He spoke to each, giving a small compliment. He noted the astonishment on the face of the lady who had fascinated him from the first and wondered at it, but the organist had begun the first hymn and he was unable to inquire about it.

The service went along as all are wont to do. Darcy noted the youngest girls with their heads together a time or two, but their behavior was exemplary, on the whole. He was pleased to see it, for it meant they were not beyond redemption.

As the last notes of the recessional faded away, Darcy and his party, as well as the Bennets, made their way out of the building, stopping to greet the rector along the way. Once freed of the restraints required in the sacred confines of the church, Lydia and Kitty felt free to put their heads together, point, and giggle at will. Darcy shook his head as he watched. *They are certainly lively.* He turned his attention to Mrs. Bennet, who had begun speaking to Bingley.

"Do say you will dine with us this evening. Surely you would like to spend more time with Jane, now that you have been reunited." The matron clutched her hands together as she looked expectantly up into Bingley's face.

"I would very much like to." Bingley turned and addressed his sister. "Caroline, do you have any objections?"

The youngest Bingley's features pinched as though she had sucked on a lemon. "I thought we could spend the afternoon at rest, but I suppose it will not hurt anything to visit Longbourn instead."

Zoe Burton

Bingley examined Caroline closely. "You do look a bit peaked. Tell you what, Darcy and I will go to Longbourn and you can go home and rest. Louisa and Hurst will not mind accompanying you, I am sure?"

At her sister's words, Louisa had also scrutinized Caroline's demeanor. "I will. She can clearly use a nice nap, and perhaps a tonic." She hooked her arm into Caroline's. "Come then, Sister. We will have you right as rain in no time."

Caroline repressed the desire to roll her eyes. She sighed to herself as her sister led her away. She was torn between wishing to closely monitor her brother's interactions with "that family" and wishing to be as far away from them as possible. Her feelings, however, required expression, so the trip back to Netherfield was filled with her objections to and disparagement of every Bennet she had met.

~~~***~~~

At Longbourn, Darcy and Bingley settled into the drawing room to visit with the ladies. As had happened the day before, Darcy was largely tongue tied when in Elizabeth's vicinity. He was not often near her, though, because she always moved to the other side of the room when he approached. Though he continued to tell himself it did not matter because he could never pursue her, he was unable to control himself. He often found himself drawing near to her or watching her.

Elizabeth did not fail to notice Darcy's attention to her and her conversations. It seemed that every time she turned around, he was either within arm's reach of her or staring at her from the other side of the room. *What is he about,* she wondered to herself. *Why does he watch me so? Am I so ugly that he must stare? Is he looking at me to find fault, the way I saw him do to Lydia and Kitty?* With this thought, her conscience reminded her of his compliments to her sisters in recent days. She frowned at the embroidery in her hands, diligently plying the needle up and down as she pondered. *He glared so fiercely at Lydia and Kitty the day he met them, then the next, he is complimenting Mary's playing and the day after that, gives each of us some very pretty words.* She glanced up to note him staring again, from a chair near to the table where she was seated, then looked back down, shaking her head. *Today, he is frowning again. I do not know what to make of him.*

Elizabeth was given further food for thought when she witnessed Darcy engaging Kitty in conversation. Though she kept her eyes on her needlework, her ears were busily eavesdropping on their words.

"Do you enjoy drawing, Miss Catherine?"

Kitty looked up, brows raised in surprise. She smiled. "I do, though I could be better if I practiced more."

"May I see?" Darcy gestured to the paper Kitty had before her.

"You may." Kitty readily handed the drawing over. She bit her lip as he examined it.

"This is your sister and my friend." Darcy looked up and caught Kitty's nod. "It is very like them. You have done well catching their expressions."

Kitty blushed at the praise. "Thank you." She hesitated. "Do you draw?"

Darcy shook his head. "Sadly, I do not. It has been years since I attempted it, and the results were poor, indeed. They rather looked like something a young child would do. My sister is very good, though. She is not as talented at drawing people as you are, but she is an excellent landscape artist."

"You have a sister? How old is she?"

"She is four and ten."

"The same age as Lydia, then." Kitty tilted her head to examine him. "Is she lively?"

Darcy hesitated. "She has been in the past. She ... she suffered a frightening experience this past summer that seems to have forced her to mature quickly." He paused. "She used to laugh loudly and run all over the house and think of everything as an adventure. She did not wish to listen when she was corrected for her behavior." He fell silent.

42

"What happened to her?" Kitty's brow furrowed.

"She went to the park with her governess one day and did not come home. She was kidnapped and held for ransom." Darcy hesitated when he heard Kitty gasp, but plunged ahead with the story, hoping to make an impression on her. "Thankfully, she has two guardians, myself and my cousin who is in the army, and he was able to find her quickly. She will not tell us what happened to her, what the kidnappers did to her, and she has lost her liveliness entirely. She has stopped playing and drawing. She has become a timid shell of her former self."

Kitty's hands had come up to cover her mouth. She stared at him over the top of them for a long moment, then lowered them. "She will tell you nothing?" When Darcy shook his head, she clasped her hands and drew them to her chest. "The poor girl! I should die of fright if that happened to me!" She paused for a moment. "Can you bring her here? I would be pleased to help cheer her up. I am quite certain Lydia would, as well."

Darcy lifted his hands. "I do not know if I will be here long enough for her to visit, or if she will feel safe enough to even make the trip, but I will write to her and ask if she would be interested in coming. Thank you for taking so much of an interest in her well-being."

"Mary always preaches to us that we should do good to others. I can see that this would be a way to do that." Kitty smiled and accepted the drawing Darcy handed back to her.

"What else does she preach to you?"

Kitty waved her hand in the air. "Oh, she is always telling us we ought to behave better and listen to Mama and do what she tells us, and that we ought to read more and talk about intelligent things instead of ribbons and boys."

"Do you think she is ever correct?" Darcy clasped his now empty hands on his lap.

Kitty opened her mouth but then closed it. She traced the images on her drawing for a moment, but then looked back at Darcy. "Yesterday, I would have said no, but after hearing about your sister, I think she may have a point."

"She very well may. It is easy to allow your desires for fun to cloud your good sense." Darcy would have said more, but Bingley hailed him from across the room and he was required to answer the call. He stood and bowed to Kitty. "Thank you for sharing your drawing, Miss Catherine, and for your conversation."

Kitty hopped up from her seat and curtseyed. "Thank you, sir."

Elizabeth's brow creased as she watched Darcy stride toward his friend. Looking back at her embroidery, she bit her lip. *If his sister is still out of spirits, it might explain his somberness and reserve. Perhaps he did not mean to look down on us,* she thought. *I have much to consider.*

Chapter 5

The gentlemen of Netherfield went out on Monday to meet some of the neighbors who were not Bennets. Of course, Bingley spent that afternoon and each day following with his betrothed. Sometimes Darcy joined him and other times not. Hurst tended to stay with his wife, who was led by her sister, though he did enjoy Mrs. Bennet's table and was always willing to take tea or dine at Longbourn.

The ladies of Netherfield remained home on Monday while their brother paved the way for them to meet the ladies of the area. Their turn to pay calls came on Tuesday, and on Wednesday, the neighborhood ladies returned the courtesy.

Caroline had hoped to uncover some sort of scandal involving the Bennets during these visits, or at least opinions that did not paint them in the best light. However, it seemed that everywhere they went, the family was universally approved.

"I cannot believe," Caroline exclaimed once the door had shut on their last guest, "that not one single person had anything bad to say about that family."

Louisa sat, settling her skirts around her. "Very surprising," she murmured.

Caroline snorted. "Surprising is an understatement. The worst anyone had to say was that Miss Lydia Bennet is lively. How can a family that large not have at least one scandal attached to their name? Not even a hint of one!"

Louisa shrugged. "They are one of the premier families in the area."

"Be that as it may, they are not high enough." Caroline began to pace. "If only Mr. Darcy would agree with me and persuade Charles to abandon Miss Bennet, we could leave this place and never return."

"That is the material point. He does not agree, and Hurst shares his opinion. Do you really wish for our name to be dragged through the mud because of a scandal of our own?" Louisa sat erect, watching her sister's movements, hands clasped in her lap.

Caroline rolled her eyes and fell back into a nearby chair. "I suppose not." She paused. "However, Mr. Darcy appears to be falling into the same trap our brother has, and that cannot happen. I intend for the next mistress of Pemberley to be me, not Miss Eliza Bennet."

"I think you are worried for nothing. They hardly speak." Keeping her eyes on Caroline, Louisa began to play with the bracelets on one hand with the fingers of the other.

"He stares at her nearly constantly! Surely you have seen it."

"She does not return his looks, though. If I do not miss my guess, she avoids him. Certainly, she walks away when he approaches."

Caroline flattened her lips. "Perhaps she does, but it has not stopped the staring."

Louisa's hands stilled once more as she addressed her sister. "I really do not think you have anything to worry about. If she dislikes him, as it appears she does, he will get nowhere with her."

"I do not like his attention being drawn by anyone but me." Caroline's lip pushed out. "What does he see in her, anyway? I remind him over and over of her lack of fashion and accomplishments." She shook her head. "I do not understand why he would even *want* to watch her."

A noise in the hall informed the ladies of the arrival of the gentlemen. They stood and waited for the men to enter the drawing room where they were located.

"We have returned!" Bingley strode into the room, approaching his sisters to give each a kiss on the cheek. "We were invited to stay for dinner, but Mrs. Bennet was forgiving when I told her I promised you I would eat at home this night. She extended another invitation for tomorrow, which I accepted on everyone's behalf."

"Really, Charles." Caroline huffed. "I wish you would consult me before you do that. I may have had other plans."

"I knew you did not, because I asked you this morning, so do not give me that." Bingley's countenance darkened. "Regardless of your desires, I am to marry Jane, and I very much look forward to it. I will spend as much time with her as I can, and frankly, I wish I could spend all my time there. Mrs. Bennet may be loud at times, but she is welcoming." He turned on his heel and stalked to the door. "Stay here tomorrow if you do not wish to dine with the Bennets. I will make some excuse or other." He skirted around his friends. "Excuse me, gentlemen. I am going to my rooms." With that, he disappeared behind the door, which he slammed shut.

Darcy darted a look toward the ladies. He opened his mouth to make his own excuses when Caroline pleaded for his attention.

"Surely you do not wish to spend any more time than necessary with such an uncouth group of people, Mr. Darcy. Can you not speak to my brother and plead our case?"

Darcy sighed to himself even as his spine stiffened. "I am sorry, but as I have told you repeatedly, your brother has signed a contract with the Bennets to marry their eldest daughter. Miss Bennet is a beautiful woman, inside and out, as are her mother and sisters. They may not be to your tastes, but they are a fine family, and I have hope that the youngest girls will mature rather quickly. By the time Miss Lydia is out in another year or two, she may very well be a poised and elegant young lady. They are certainly entertaining; I am never bored visiting Longbourn." He hesitated. "In any case, I do not object to the family at all at this point. There is no point to it. Bingley will marry Miss Bennet and become your sister. It is time you accepted the fact and left him alone about it."

Caroline's features had twisted as Darcy spoke, her skin becoming redder the longer he did. Though she clenched her jaw in an effort to hold her affront inside, it would not be subdued. "Really, Mr. Darcy! One would think you were as enamored of a Bennet as my brother is. What can you be thinking? None of them are accomplished to any great degree. They do not speak the refined languages, they paint no screens, there is nothing about their air or manner of walking that sets them apart from the common. In short, there is nothing to recommend any of them. Charles may be marrying into the family, but it does not follow that I must treat them any better than they deserve."

Louisa's gasp at the beginning of this speech had been ignored. Now, she stood and gripped Caroline's arm. "Sister!" She turned to Darcy. "Please, sir, forgive her. I do not know what has come over her to speak so to you, a guest in our home."

Darcy had stood even stiffer and more erect the longer Caroline spoke. His mien darkened, becoming a forbidding mask. Without a word, when Louisa was finished speaking, he bowed and spun on his heel, exiting the room and heading to his chambers.

The drawing room remained silent except for Caroline's heaving breaths. After a long moment, Hurst cleared his throat. "Come, Wife. I desire your company upstairs." He turned slightly toward the door and extended his elbow.

Louisa hesitated, torn between her sister and her spouse. After a heartbeat or two, she reluctantly let go of Caroline's arm and walked over to Hurst, allowing him to escort her out.

Caroline stood in the center of the drawing room for several minutes, rage keeping her still and rigid. Finally, with an angry screech, she began to stride to the door, pausing at a small table beside one of the chairs to seize the figurine placed there and throw it with all her might against the wall. Then, she marched out of the room and up the stairs. Alone.

In his bedchamber, Darcy paced angrily back and forth from the bed to the fireplace. He slashed his arm through the air as if to punctuate his thoughts. *Who does Caro-*

line Bingley think she is to speak to me so? She is neither my mother, my sister, nor, thank goodness, my wife. He made a couple more trips back and forth in silence and then suddenly stopped.

"She wishes to marry me. Why have I not seen this before?" Darcy put his hands to his head, running them back and forth through his hair. "That will be the day! I would not marry her if she were the last woman in the world." He shuddered at the thought of being tied for life to his friend's harsh and scheming sister. "Never!"

A knock on the dressing room door made him turn around. "Yes?"

Mr. Smith, Darcy's valet, stood in the doorway. "I have had water brought up for washing." He glanced at the clock. "I believe dinner will be served in one hour."

With a sharp nod, Darcy acknowledged Smith's words. Reaching up to untie his cravat, he began walking toward the doorway as the servant stepped back to allow him entrance.

Darcy said nothing as he washed up and changed his clothing. His mind was turning over his realization. Suddenly, he spoke. "I wish for you to keep the doors to my rooms locked at all times while we are at Netherfield."

Smith immediately consented. That he did not seem surprised by such a request set Darcy back on his heels.

"I get the feeling you may have been waiting for me to ask this specific thing." He watched the valet carefully as the man tied a perfect, fashionable knot in the fresh cravat around Darcy's neck.

Smith shrugged. "I confess I have, sir."

Darcy was silent for a long moment. "What led you to believe I might?"

The servant fussed with his master's cufflinks. "Rumors abound in any household, as I am certain you already know. 'Tis no secret here that Miss Bingley has set her cap at you. She is known to be devious." He looked up, into his employer's eyes. "I was warned that no arts were beyond her; she will use whatever weapon is at her disposal to gain that which she desires."

Darcy looked thoughtful. "I cannot believe a lady with Miss Bingley's training and elegance would stoop to such a thing, but it is better to be safe than sorry, is it not?" With another nod to his valet, he turned and left the room. Smith followed him to the hallway door, firmly turning the key in the lock.

Lucas Lodge, two days later ...

Darcy followed Bingley and his family into the home of Sir William Lucas, the former mayor of Meryton and now unofficial greeter of newcomers. He had spent much of the day reminding himself of the reasons he could not pursue Elizabeth and being determined to avoid her, as she had clearly avoided him in recent days. He now kept his gaze fixed firmly on his host as introductions were made to that gentleman's wife and eldest daughters.

Immediately upon the completion of those items of politeness, Darcy retired to the formal parlor at the front of the house, where the rest of the guests were waiting. Darcy could see as he circulated the edges of the room that a wall had been removed to enlarge the space, making it and the room next door into one larger, rectangular room. Having noted the absence of the Bennets on his circuit, he breathed a sigh of relief. He accepted a glass of wine from a passing footman and did his best to fade into the woodwork and hold up the wall.

It was not long, however, before the Bennet ladies were announced. Darcy stiffened when he heard their names. He swallowed and tossed back the remainder of the dark red liquid in his glass. Though he did his best to keep his eyes firmly in the opposite direction from where Elizabeth's warm laughter could be heard gurgling out of her throat, when she passed by with Charlotte Lucas, his gaze was arrested by the sight of her in her elegant lavender gown.

From across the room, Caroline Bingley noted Darcy's behavior and seethed silently. Squaring her shoulders, she made her way to his side, standing as close as she dared. "I know what you must be thinking," she murmured to him.

Upon hearing Caroline's voice in his ear, Darcy rolled his eyes before he could stop himself. He turned his head to look at her, being careful to keep his eyes on her face. "I doubt that very much."

Caroline blinked, not having expected such a response. She quickly recovered, however. "You and I are much alike. We have been of the same mind on many occasions in similar situations. I believe you are wondering what you could be doing here, among such insipid people at such an insignificant gathering."

Darcy's mask of indifference grew tighter, his lips pressing together and his chin rising higher. "Indeed not." He looked out at the growing crowd of people. "I was instead considering other, more pleasant things. I was thinking about the way fine eyes will turn a merely pretty woman into the most beautiful creature I have ever beheld."

Flattering herself that he thought of her in such a way, Caroline flushed, a small smile of triumph lifting the corners of her mouth. "Indeed? And who, pray tell, is the recipient of such praise?" She fluttered her fan as her heart sped up.

"Miss Elizabeth Bennet."

Caroline's eyes narrowed. She followed Darcy's gaze and noted that it rested upon Elizabeth. She was silent for a few moments as she struggled to retain control of her temper. When she felt able to speak, she spent a good quarter hour slyly jabbing her brother's friend with his good fortune in having such an enjoyable and quiet mother-in-law. It was only when she realized that she was not going to get a response from him that she left off, abandoning him entirely. She retreated to Louisa's side to reconnoiter and decide what her next steps would be.

Chapter 6

Darcy winced internally when he spoke Elizabeth's name to Caroline before he thought better of it. Then, he shrugged to himself. *Oh, well,* he thought. *It is easy enough to tune her out when I wish to.* He stood silently, hearing her mockery of his future with just half an ear. *If only you knew, Caroline. I am well aware that Elizabeth does not meet the expectations required of a lady looking to be my wife.* Though his head knew this to be true, his heart ached at the thought.

Thankfully for Darcy, the meal was announced. As the highest ranking guest, he escorted his hostess into the dining room, sitting to her right. Darcy was, as always, quiet but observant. Thankfully for his composure, he could not see Elizabeth from his position, though he heard her warm gurgle of laughter every now and again.

~~~***~~~

Caroline was also largely silent. She was seated nearer to Sir William than she liked, and was between two gentlemen of the neighborhood: Mr. Goulding and Mr. Long. She was happy to note that Darcy and Elizabeth were on opposite ends of the table and on the same side, for it meant they could not converse at all.

"How do you like our fair hamlet, Miss Bingley?" Mr. Long, a gentleman of middling years with graying blond hair, inquired from her right.

Swallowing down the harsh words she would have liked to use, Caroline smiled and prevaricated. "It is lovely. A very pretty part of England ... you should be proud of it."

Mr. Long beamed. "I am, indeed, proud of it." He gestured around the table. "Most of us here are. I, for one, would not wish to live anywhere else. We are conveniently placed, being so close to London and to the turnpike. A trip to town is nothing at all. Not like being in one of the further counties."

Caroline had nothing to say to that, and so simply smiled. Thankfully, the attention of her dinner partners was drawn in other directions, and she was left to ruminate once more. It was not until the ladies separated from the gentlemen that the kernel of an idea came to her as a method of coming between Darcy and Elizabeth.

Caroline watched her rival as the other girl chattered with friends and made her way around the room. When she saw Elizabeth stop at the fireplace and admire the screen, she seized her chance and approached.

"Good evening, Miss Eliza." Caroline curtseyed shallowly as Elizabeth did the same.

"Good evening. I hope you are enjoying yourself. Lady Lucas and Sir William love to entertain." A small lift of Elizabeth's lips accompanied her words.

Caroline sniffed. "I am. Lady Lucas sets a fine table." She paused. "I noticed Mr. Darcy paying close attention to you earlier. I wanted to warn you, as your friend, not to give it more meaning than you should. His affections are ..." Caroline glanced down as though suddenly shy. "Engaged elsewhere." She looked up. "I should hate for you to be disappointed when he does not offer for you."

A long pause accompanied her words. She watched as a strange look passed over Elizabeth's face. She could not tell what it meant.

"Is that so?" Elizabeth took a sip out of the glass of wine in her hand. "I had not noticed Mr. Darcy paying me any more attention than he has anyone else, so I can assure you I am not expecting his addresses. I thank you, though, for the warning. It was quite ... kind of you to do so."

Caroline's features sharpened. She was uncertain from Elizabeth's tone of voice if she was being serious or facetious. Deciding for now to assume she was the former, Caroline chose to be gracious. "It was the least I could do. I would hate for *my* hopes to be dashed and would feel horrible to be the cause of that state for another." With a lift of her chin, she curtseyed again. "In case I do not get another opportunity to say it, good evening." She turned and walked away.

Elizabeth watched Caroline make her way to her sister's side with a crease between her brows. *I wonder what brought that on? Surely she does not think Mr. Darcy likes me!* She shook her head. *What a strange person she is.* She turned back to the screen she had been admiring, one of Charlotte's. As she was examining it and pondering Caroline's words, that exact friend strolled up to stand beside her.

"Are you enjoying yourself, Lizzy?"

Elizabeth turned toward Charlotte with a warm smile. "I am. Your parents always have such entertaining parties."

"Mother worried over the duck, but everyone seems to have liked it. There was nothing left of it, in any event."

"What does she have planned for entertainment?" Elizabeth tipped her head as she looked at her friend. For a second, her eyes darted past the other woman's shoulder to where Caroline sat with Louisa. A frown passed momentarily over her lips, but then she returned her attention to Charlotte with a smile.

"Cards, mostly, but Maria has been begging for dancing and you know Mother will allow it."

Elizabeth chuckled. "She will, but I think all of us would. Who does not like to dance?"

A commotion at the door caused both ladies to turn. Sir William led the gentlemen of the party into the room. Elizabeth noted the way in which they each seemed to gravitate toward a particular woman, except Darcy. She watched him walk to a window and look out into the gathering darkness.

"He watches you quite a bit." Charlotte spoke as she moved to face her friend once more.

Elizabeth's brows rose to her hairline. "Who?"

Charlotte raised her own brows. "Why, Mr. Darcy, of course. Who did you think I was referring to?"

With a blink, Elizabeth closed her mouth, which had fallen open. "I had not the slightest notion."

"Well, he does. Every time I see him, especially at Longbourn, he is staring at you. I think he likes you."

Elizabeth shook her head. "You are wrong. You were not there the first time he met us. He frowned quite fiercely at us all."

Charlotte shrugged. "I did not see it, so I can only assume you are correct. However, if he dislikes you all, how do you explain his compliments on Sunday, and his recent discussion with Kitty?"

"You know about that?" Elizabeth's voice rose slightly.

"Yes, Kitty told Lydia, who then told Maria. I overheard the three of them talking about it yesterday. Whatever he said, it made an impact on at least one."

"Hmm." Elizabeth's brows drew together again. She searched the room until she located her sisters and Maria, sitting on a sofa with their heads together. "They have been rather quiet, have they not?"

"They have. With soldiers in the room, no less."

"How interesting," Elizabeth murmured as she watched the three girls rise as one and approach Darcy.

~~~***~~~

Darcy stood at the drawing room window for several minutes. He required some time to mentally prepare himself for seeing Elizabeth again. He turned, eventually, and when a footman brought him a cup of tea, he accepted it. His gaze searched the long room, observing the other guests and who was sitting with whom. He noted Elizabeth's youngest sisters and another girl who he believed to be a daughter of his hosts, sitting together. Suddenly, they rose together and approached him.

"Good evening, Mr. Darcy." Kitty curtseyed, the other young ladies following suit. "I hope you do not mind, but I shared a bit of our conversation with my sister and Maria."

Darcy bowed to each of the young ladies. "I do not mind at all. What did your friends think of what you told them?"

Lydia, never one to sit back and allow someone else to speak for her, asked him their first question. "Is it true that your sister was kidnapped?"

Darcy's reply was solemn. "It is."

"And she was greatly affected by it?" Lydia's eyes had widened as she glanced at her sister and friend. "What could cause such alteration?"

"She was and still is. She would not tell us of the events, of what was done to her, so I can only suppose it was terribly frightening. Georgiana was never so timid before."

The third girl, whom Darcy still only knew as a Lucas girl, whispered, "It must have been awful." In a louder voice, she put forth a question of her own. "Was she kidnapped because she was lively?"

"No." Darcy shook his head. "She was kidnapped because she is an heiress. However, her liveliness meant that she did not pay attention to her surroundings, or to the behavior of those around her. One of the servants was involved, and had Georgiana been paying attention, she would have noticed the signs that this woman was not as she seemed to be. She would have been able to alert me, and I could have taken steps to prevent the incident. Being lively is good. Being so lively that you ignore what you know to be right often leads to danger."

Lydia tossed her head. "I am not an heiress. No one would ever kidnap me." Just as she finished speaking, a raucous round of laughter burst forth out of a cluster of soldiers at one end of the room.

"You are correct." Darcy tipped his head in the direction of the laughter. "However, there are other ways a young lady with a propensity for liveliness can find herself in trouble because of it. What do you think of those gentlemen in the red coats?"

All three young ladies turned to look at the officers. They sighed and smiled.

"They are ever so dashing!" Kitty turned back to Darcy as she spoke.

Lydia and Maria followed suit, gazing up at Darcy to see what he would say. A look of horror crossed Maria's face as a thought entered her mind.

"It was not an officer who kidnapped Miss Darcy, was it?"

Darcy shook his head. "No, it was not." He paused, uncertain how to make his point without giving the girls more information than they needed. Assuming that at fourteen and sixteen, their mothers would have warned them about allowing gentlemen to take liberties, he plunged ahead. "Not every

66

gentleman is honorable," he began. "Many will whisper pretty words and promises in a young lady's ear, hoping to persuade her to give him favors. When the young lady gives in, the unscrupulous gentleman walks away from her, leaving her ruined."

Even Lydia's eyes had grown large at this point. All three turned again toward the soldiers, this time grabbing each other's hands.

Darcy heard Kitty whisper, "How can you tell who is honorable and who is not?"

He replied in an equally soft voice. "It is often difficult. You must listen to his conversation and observe his behavior with others. Does he flirt too much? What does he say? What is his manner? Is his flattery sincere, or is he telling you what he thinks you want to hear? If he says he wishes to court you, is he willing to go to your father and ask permission, or does he prefer to sneak around? Is he asking you to meet him alone, or is he willing to accept a chaperone?"

The ladies were quiet for a long time, brows creased. They eventually turned toward him. Kitty again spoke for her companions. "You have given us much to consider. Thank you, Mr. Darcy." She curtseyed and Maria followed suit.

"If we have more questions, may we come to you and ask?" Lydia arrested Darcy's attention with a demanding gaze.

"You may. I will be glad to speak to you at any time." Darcy bowed to the three.

"Thank you." Lydia gave her curtsey and followed her friends across the room.

Darcy felt as though a burden had been lifted from his shoulders. He did not know if his words would be accepted or if they would make a difference in the future, but for at least this night, he had given the girls some food for thought.

His attention no longer engaged, Darcy allowed his eyes to roam, locating his friend, who stood at the mantel speaking to Jane to the exclusion of everyone else. He noted the seats in which Caroline and Louisa were situated, and beyond them, he saw Elizabeth speaking to Charlotte Lucas.

"How are you enjoying the party, Mr. Darcy?" Sir William Lucas had approached his guest from the other end of the room.

"I like it very much." Darcy bowed to the other gentleman. "I appreciated the fine food and conversation."

"Capital! Capital! I will pass your compliments on to my wife. It is Lady Lucas who plans these things out, you know. She is a fine woman. Excellent housekeeper and mother, as well."

Darcy had nothing to say to this, and so remained silent. His attention was drawn to the pianoforte, where Mary Bennet and some of the other ladies had taken turns playing. Some of the gentlemen were moving furniture back.

Sir William followed his gaze. "I heard one of the Longs' nieces ask Miss Mary for music to dance to, and encouraged her to accommodate them. Dancing is an excellent way to pass the time. Have you danced at Saint James'?"

"I have, but only once." Darcy sighed to himself. He looked down, hoping the older gentleman would not press the issue. "It is not a favored pastime. Every savage can dance."

"Oh, but look here!" Sir Williams' sudden exclamation brought Darcy's head up. "Surely you cannot refuse to participate when such beauty is before you, sir."

Elizabeth blushed at her host's words. "Please do not think I came this way to beg a partner."

Darcy had not seen her approach, but with the object of his desire standing in front of him, his heart began to pound in his ears. Before he could stop himself, he heard his voice asking her a question. "May I have this set? As Sir William has said, I truly cannot refuse to dance when my partner is as lovely as you."

Elizabeth pursed her lips as she tilted her head and raised her brows. After a long pause, she shrugged. "You may."

Chapter 7

Darcy stood in silence for a long moment, hardly able to believe he had asked the object of his fascination to dance, and she had consented. With a start, he shook off his surprise, swallowed, and extended his elbow to her. When her small hand settled into the crook, he felt a flash of electricity hit his arm and travel straight to his heart. Unable to think of anything to say, he escorted Elizabeth to the line of dancers, joining in the middle of a song.

The movements of the dance passed down the line quickly in such a small gathering, and before Darcy had a chance to really brace himself, he was once again grasping her hands, this time to skip up the line. He felt frozen, his hands as icy as the solid block his brain had become. He was relieved when his partner finally spoke.

"I must say, Mr. Darcy, that I do not get on well at all in trying to sketch your character. You appear one way in one setting and present yourself as a completely different person in another." Elizabeth was quiet for a long moment, partly because the steps had separated them. She smiled distractedly at another gentleman who she briefly partnered with. When she and Darcy returned to each other, her brow creased. "Perhaps it is not my entire family you dislike, but myself alone. Certainly, you have spoken more to my younger sisters than to anyone else in my family." She huffed and shook her head. "I do not understand you, and I do not enjoy being at such a loss."

Darcy was shocked as he listened to Elizabeth speak. *Not like her,* he thought. *How did I give that impression?* He cleared his throat. "I apologize." The dance required him to partner with another lady at that point and he used the time to formulate his response to Elizabeth. When they joined hands again, he continued. "I am uncomfortable meeting new people. I did not realize I had given such an impression."

Elizabeth raised an eyebrow and pursed her lips. "A gentleman of the world, shy? It makes no sense."

Darcy let go of Elizabeth's hand to return to the gentlemen's side of the line. The music to the first dance faded away, but before anyone could move, the next song began. He raised his voice slightly, to be heard across the space and over the music and other voices. "I have not the talent that I see in others to speak freely to new acquaintances. I cannot catch the tone of their conversations or share in their interests." He began to feel defensive, a new sensation in his experience. He had always been confident in himself and his place in the world. Never before had he felt a need to give an explanation for his behavior.

Though his partner continued to look skeptical, she remained silent.

Darcy cleared his throat as he reached his hands out to Elizabeth when their turn to move down the line came. Though he thought he had braced himself, the new touch of her hand made his heart skip a beat. He waited for her next words.

"Perhaps you simply need to practice, then." Elizabeth looked up at him from the corner of her eye. "One cannot master any skill without it."

"You may be correct." He inclined his head in recognition of the truth of her words.

"What were you talking so earnestly to my sisters about?"

The sudden change of subject made Darcy's mind spin for a moment. He caught himself, however, and formulated a respectable reply. "I had previously shared with Miss Catherine something that happened this past summer with my sister. Tonight, she and Miss Lydia and their friend asked for clarification." He shrugged as he stepped back to his side to await their next turn. "I happily gave it."

Elizabeth eyed Darcy speculatively. "And the pointing at the soldiers bit?"

Darcy blushed slightly and looked down. "I pointed out that not every gentleman is truly a gentleman and that a young lady must be wise in how much she listens to them."

"They accepted such a vague reply?" Doubt colored Elizabeth's tone of voice.

"No, they did not. I was required to give examples." Darcy shrugged again. "I did not become overly graphic, but I did point out that if a gentleman is not willing to court a lady in front of her family and is asking to meet her in secret, he is not a good gentleman."

Elizabeth's brows rose to her hairline for a moment. She was quiet as she digested this information. "Why would you do such a thing?"

"I noticed their liveliness and wished to do what I could to spare them heartaches in the future." Darcy fell quiet for a moment, and then finished with a bitter, "Would that I had done so for my own sister."

It was Elizabeth's turn to be quiet. "I am sorry that your sister, and by extension you, have gone through what must have been a very painful episode."

The second dance ended with Darcy and Elizabeth standing on their respective sides. He bowed and she curtseyed.

"Thank you, Miss Elizabeth. May I escort you somewhere? To your friend or your mother, or the punch bowl?"

Elizabeth smiled. "You may escort me to the punch, if you please. Thank you for the dances. They were lovely."

In silence, the couple strolled to the other end of the room, where Lady Lucas had a small bowl of punch set up, along with a tea service. Darcy requested two cups of the lukewarm lemonade and berry liquid, handing one to his partner.

In an effort to begin a conversation, since the pair of them stood together, Elizabeth asked Darcy a question. "Are you enjoying the entertainment?"

"I am." Darcy cleared his throat. "It is not quite what I am used to, with the younger children taking an active part, but as I told Sir William, I have found the meal and the conversation to be entertaining. Now I can add to that the dancing. When one has an excellent partner, the activity is much more enjoyable."

Elizabeth colored and looked down, but only briefly. She raised her chin almost immediately and looked Darcy in the eye. "And when one's partner is not a complete stranger?"

It was Darcy's turn to blush. The corner of his lip turned down and he sketched a shallow bow, but the frown twisted into a small smirk. "Yes, ma'am."

Elizabeth shook her head. She opened her mouth to say something when a young man approached. He did not appear to be much older than four and ten.

"Miss Elizabeth, may I have this dance?"

Darcy watched as a soft smile joined the twinkle in Elizabeth's eyes.

"You may, Master Lucas." Elizabeth turned to Darcy. "Thank you again for the dances, and the conversation. You have given me much to contemplate." She curtseyed and then accepted the Lucas boy's arm and walked away.

A feeling roared through Darcy at the sight of Elizabeth strolling off on the arm of another, an unfamiliar emotion that he could not easily identify. Whatever it was, he knew it was rooted in his dislike of another gentleman – or, in this case, boy – receiving her undivided attention. *Calm down, man,* he told himself. *It will happen one day soon, regardless. Accept it for what it is and be grateful.*

~~~***~~~

Darcy relived that feeling many times over the next few days. No matter how often he told himself that Elizabeth, despite her manifold attractions, was not the sort of woman he could marry and still do his duty to his sister and his family name, he could not get her out of his mind. Worse, he began to chafe at the expectations he knew his family held. He started to see them as restrictions and grew angry.

No matter how many long rides he took, lathering his horse and his person with their vigor, no matter how many books he tried to lose himself in, or how many games of cards or billiards he played with Bingley and Hurst, he could not get Elizabeth out of his mind. She had even begun invading his dreams, causing him to wake with a longing for her presence that would not be soothed. He had avoided visits to Longbourn, claiming he had correspondence to attend to, but it did not help. Everywhere he turned, she was there, at least in his mind.

To further aggravate the situation, Caroline continued to press her attentions onto him. No matter how brusque he became or how many warnings her brother gave her, she made sure his focus was on her as much as possible. Darcy and his valet continued to keep the doors to his rooms locked. He was certain he heard the knob turn in the night at least once.

Though he did his best to hide his feelings, Darcy was aware that they were seeping into his interactions with his friends.

~~~***~~~

At Longbourn, Darcy occupied far more of Elizabeth's thoughts than she imagined was wise. She longed to speak to her favorite sister about it, but Jane was wrapped up in wedding plans and Bingley. She was cross with herself, though, and knew she must express herself to someone, so she was grateful one afternoon when she and Mary were playing chaperone in the garden for their sister and her betrothed, and Mary inquired of her.

"I know that you and Jane are close and share everything," Mary began, "but you seem to have something on your mind and Jane is preoccupied." She blushed and her gaze faltered for a moment, but then she looked back up at Elizabeth. "I am not Jane, but perhaps I can help you, even if it is only to allow you to think out loud. I am not Lydia. I will not tell anyone what you share with me."

Elizabeth caught her breath, lifting her fingers to cover her lips. She lowered them and reached for her sister's arm. "Oh, Mary, do forgive me! There *is* something on my mind. I would have approached you earlier, but I feared you would not be interested in my concerns."

Mary flushed a little, but shrugged. "In the past, I might not have been, but ..." She tipped her head toward her eldest sister and Bingley. "Things are changing at Longbourn and it occurred to me that our ... positions, maybe ... might change. You will soon be the eldest unmarried Bennet daughter, and the household will lose its most serene member and the one best able to manage Mama. I have always been the odd one, being in the middle; it has caused me to forge my own path, so to speak." She straightened her shoulders. "I believe it is time for me to set that aside, and if I can be a better sister to you, I would like to do it." She added softly, "It would be nice to have a sister I am close to, as well."

Elizabeth squeezed Mary's arm and smiled. "I would like that." She threw her arms around the other girl for a hug, then separated again. She began to explain what was happening with Darcy. When she finished, she was astonished at her sister's insight.

"I suspect Charlotte is correct. I, too, have seen Mr. Darcy staring at you."

"You have?" Elizabeth's eyes grew wide. "But ... he frowned so fiercely at Kitty and Lydia the first day he visited!"

"He also complimented all of us, including Mama, at church. He praised my proficiency in playing, too. No one has ever done that before, at least not since my last music master left us. And, did you not tell me that his sister went through some sort of horrible event this past summer? Is it possible she was on his mind that first day?"

"Well, yes, it is. I have thought so myself a time or two, though I do tend to forget the timing of the events." Elizabeth blushed a deep red. She put her hands to her cheeks. "I am so embarrassed about that. He is far stronger than I to have been calmly visiting strangers after one of my sisters was kidnapped and came back an entirely different person."

"I agree. I could not have done it, but it seems to have done some good." At Elizabeth's perplexed look, Mary reminded her of the talks Darcy had participated in with their youngest sisters. "They have stopped talking of officers so much. Perhaps Mr. Darcy was able to influence them in a manner you, Jane, and I have never been able to."

Elizabeth nodded, biting her lip. "Perhaps he has. So, you are saying that I should stop avoiding him and assign to him a good character?"

"I am." Mary watched her sister closely. "What are you thinking now?"

Elizabeth sighed, looking down at her hands, clasped in her lap. "When he first entered our home, I thought him the most handsome gentleman I had ever beheld, but what is the likelihood of a match being made between us? His standing is far above ours." She paused, remembering Caroline's implication. "Miss Bingley told me his affections are already engaged."

"I am not sure I would trust everything Miss Bingley says. She behaves as though she is better than us." Mary shook her head. "It is very un-Christian of her to do so. I think if Mr. Darcy loved you and you loved him, social standing would not matter."

Elizabeth was quiet for a few minutes; Mary allowed her time to contemplate. When they had trailed Jane and Bingley back to the house, the younger girls embraced.

"Thank you, Mary. Your insights were helpful to me." Elizabeth pulled back, but kept her arms around her sister. "I think I am going to enjoy having you for a confidant."

Mary's beaming smile lit her entire countenance. Arms linked, they followed the betrothed couple into the warmth of Longbourn's entry hall.

Chapter 8

The following days were busy ones for the ladies of Longbourn. Elizabeth still took her walks and found time to contemplate Darcy and the conundrum he represented. She often wished she could speak to her father about it, but her mother had decreed that he was to be left alone at all costs; none were to disturb him or cut up his peace. Elizabeth doubted he would be disturbed in any negative fashion by such a discussion, but she supposed that since laughter might increase his heart rate as much as anger would, she should keep it all to herself.

Eventually, the night of the monthly Meryton assembly ball arrived. Elizabeth found herself dressing with extra care.

"I do not know why," she said to Mary. "It is not as though there is anyone to care."

"You will care, and that is enough." Mary watched as the maid put the finishing touches on her sister's hair. "I daresay, though, that you will turn many heads, including that of Mr. Darcy."

Elizabeth rolled her eyes but chuckled. "Oh, Mary, you are good for my vanity. Thank you for the compliment, and for your faith in me."

Mary shrugged. "It is nothing you would not do for me."

"Very true." Elizabeth thanked the maid just in time to hear her mother call for the girl. "I will take care of my sister's hair. You may go." She watched as the servant curtseyed and scurried out of the room, then stood.

"Come, Mary. You take my seat." She reached for the brush as her sister obeyed. "You always wear your hair in such a severe fashion … what say we give you a coiffure with a bit of daring?" Elizabeth winked, then giggled when Mary looked uncertain.

~~~***~~~

At Netherfield, Darcy paced his dressing room. Bingley insisted the entire party accompany him to Meryton for an assembly. Bingley, of course, was picking Jane up from Longbourn first, leaving his friend to accompany his family. *At least there are an equal number of gentlemen and ladies in the party,* he thought. *Hurst and I can sit together on one seat and Caroline and Louisa can do the same on the other.* He shuddered at the thought of having to sit that close to Bingley's unmarried sister.

The seating arrangements in the carriage were not what caused him to pace, however. It was the thought of seeing Elizabeth again.

Darcy had accompanied his friend to Longbourn twice in the past week. Each time, he had been drawn to the second Bennet daughter like a bee to a flower. To his surprise, she seemed to have stopped avoiding him, instead smiling warmly at him. He sat beside her at each visit, largely tongue-tied. Thankfully, she was willing to begin the conversations. He spent several enjoyable hours in her company.

Darcy was surprised how comfortable he was with Elizabeth. He did not know anyone else outside of his family with whom he felt so easy. He realized with a start as he left Longbourn one day that his perpetual loneliness had been banished while at her side.

Now, as he walked back and forth in his rooms, attempting to expend some excess energy, he was both eager to be in Elizabeth's presence again and dreading it. He stopped in the middle, oblivious to the surreptitious looks his valet cast him. He closed his eyes, breathing in deeply as his conscience warred with his desires. In the end, he knew there was but one thing to do. His eyes popped open. *I will grasp this night and cherish her to the full, and to Hades with the consequences. Tomorrow I can go back to avoiding her.* His course for the evening now set, Darcy gave a firm nod and strode out of the room.

An hour later, when the carriage pulled up at the assembly hall, Darcy burst out of it before the footman could lower the step. He was eager to see Elizabeth and secure a set, but he was also happy to be out of the equipage and Caroline's fawning presence.

"Go on inside. I will escort the ladies; no need for both of us to be tortured."

Darcy looked at Hurst to see if he was serious, and, when the other gentleman nodded toward the door with a smirk, breathed a sigh of relief. "Thank you." He turned away and hurried up the steps and into the building.

Inside, he immediately spotted Bingley, Jane, and the rest of the Bennet ladies standing in a group. He approached, bowing to his friend and each lady. He made sure to compliment them, as well, a warm feeling filling him as he noted Elizabeth's approval. Finally, the social niceties observed, he stopped in front of his favorite Bennet.

"Is your first set taken, Miss Elizabeth?"

Elizabeth's brows rose. "No, it is not."

"May I have it, then?" Darcy's mouth went dry as he awaited her response.

"You may." Elizabeth's warm smile accompanied her words, along with the twinkling of her eyes.

"Thank you." Darcy bowed, nearly sighing in relief. He could not keep a smile from spreading over his face. "Would you like to walk around the room with me while we wait for the dancing to begin?"

"I would." Elizabeth tucked her hand in the crook of his elbow, then looked to Mary, who stood beside her. "Will you be well by yourself for a bit?"

Before Mary could reply, Darcy invited her to walk with them. "I would not at all mind escorting you, as well, Miss Mary, if you wish to join us."

With a smile and a blush, Mary declined. "No, no, you go ahead. I will be well here with my sisters. Thank you for offering, though."

"Very well, then." Elizabeth touched Mary's hand. "We will likely pass by at least once; if you change your mind, we would be happy for you to join us."

Darcy felt all the comfort of Elizabeth's touch as they began to stroll into the ballroom and around to the left. He imagined what it would be like to have that feeling always. His heart swelled. Though his duty poked at the back of his mind, he forcefully shoved it away, determined to seize this one night and then cherish the memory forever.

As the couple ambled along, they began to converse. Darcy had been delighted to discover previously that Elizabeth shared his tastes in music and books. Now, they discussed the decorations and architecture of the assembly hall. He was relieved to find that his partner disliked ostentation and preferred understated elegance. As they stopped periodically to speak to one or another acquaintance, he was also happy to note that she quite easily engaged others in small talk and just as easily disengaged them from the activity. The more time they spent, the further into love with her he fell.

Finally, the musicians switched from practice tones to an organized melody. Darcy led Elizabeth to the dance floor, leaving her on the ladies' side and stepping across to take his place with the other gentlemen. When the figure was called and the steps began, there was little conversation between him and his partner. He, for one, was too caught up in the delight of it to speak, and it seemed as though she might be, as well, judging by the blushes and smiles she bestowed upon him.

On the other side of the ballroom, Caroline Bingley watched the object of her obsession dance through narrowed eyes. *This will not do,* she thought. *Clearly, warning Miss Eliza of a previous attachment did nothing.* She vowed to herself to come up with something more severe.

Though Caroline danced, none of her sets were claimed by Darcy, even after she had stood next to him for a full half hour and dropped obvious hints. She was fully aware that he was too clever to have missed her intent, which meant he was purposely ignoring her. Her anger grew.

Then, she spotted him dancing with Elizabeth a second time, this time engaging the other woman in an intense and seemingly flirtatious conversation. Her rage increased.

"Caroline! What is wrong with you?" Louisa shook her sister's arm. "You were quite rude to Sir William just now. He said nothing offensive; nothing that should cause you to snap at him so."

Caroline pulled her arm out of Louisa's grasp. "Nothing is wrong with me," she snarled. "Leave me alone."

Louisa set her jaw. She stretched up to hiss into her slightly taller sister's ear. "I will not. Your behavior is shameful and I will not have it. Sir William is not the first person to suffer your tongue tonight and I will know why."

Caroline whipped around and stared at her eldest sibling, jaw clenched and lips pressed into a line. "What do you mean, you 'will not have it'? I am an adult and will do as I please."

"You are a minor and will obey your elders. Tell me what is wrong and change your behavior or we will leave this assembly and spend the rest of the evening at home. Alone."

Caroline stared for a long moment, not a word passing her lips. It was unusual for Louisa to take such a stand nowadays, though she had on occasion when they were younger. Caroline considered ignoring her sibling and walking away, but knew she was serious. Finally, she blew a breath out of her nose and unclenched her jaw enough to speak. "I saw something that upset me." She turned and gestured to the dance floor. "Mr. Darcy is dancing again with Miss Elizabeth Bennet. I have warned both of them repeatedly against forming an attachment and yet, there they are."

"Hm. Well, I do not know what you think being angry about it is going to do." Louisa paused, eyeing her sister with skepticism. "I am certain Mr. Darcy would never offer for Miss Elizabeth and that your warnings were taken seriously. You should relax and enjoy the evening. Smile, show the ladies here what an accomplished woman looks and behaves like, and be gracious. Perhaps someone will even ask you to dance. But Caroline ..." She paused again, looking her sister in the eye. "Any more rude behavior out of you and I will take you home, if I have to get our brother over here to back me up. Do you understand?"

Caroline rolled her eyes. "Yes, Louisa, I do." She then proceeded to ignore her sister, watching the rest of the set of dances and mentally listing the steps she could take to put a stop to any romance between the man she intended to marry and Miss Elizabeth Bennet.

~~~***~~~

It would be much later that night – the next morning, really – before Caroline thought of the perfect plan. Once the party had returned to Netherfield after the assembly and had separated to their chambers, Caroline had prepared for bed still reviewing her mental list. Her ablutions complete, she dismissed the maid and climbed onto the high mattress, covering up and blowing out the candle. Just as she started to drift into sleep, she remembered Darcy's aunt, Lady Catherine de Bourgh. Her eyes popped open. "That is it! When I met her, Lady Catherine was constantly reminding Darcy of his duty. She would never condone his marriage to someone so low."

Caroline threw off the covers and hurried across the cold floor to the table near the fireplace. Taking up the candelabra sitting there, she lit it from the fire and placed it back on the table, in the center. She opened the writing desk and pulled out the supplies she needed. Swiftly, she composed a letter to Darcy's aunt. She re-read it when she was done, crossing out errors and making corrections, then wrote a clean copy on fresh paper. She sanded it, folded it, addressed it, and applied a wax seal to it. Putting her supplies away and blowing out the candles, she left the missive on the table. "I will send it express," she murmured as she climbed back into bed. She grinned in the darkness at the thought of the haughty Lady Catherine taking Elizabeth to task. Within seconds, she was asleep.

Chapter 9

Rosings Park, Kent

Lady Catherine de Bourgh accepted the express from the footman, who extended it to her in the center of a silver salver. She nodded her head one time, dismissing him, before peering at the direction on the front.

"Who is that from, Mother?" Anne de Bourgh reclined on a chaise lounge nearby.

Lady Catherine looked up from her perusal of the envelope in her hand to cast an appraising eye over her only child. "I do not know. The return direction is from somewhere in Hertfordshire." She paused. "You look pale. You have overdone again. I told you driving lessons would be too much." She sniffed and looked back at her letter. "You would not listen and now here you lie."

Anne rolled her eyes. "I did not overdo. The lesson was only a half hour in length and I was bundled up to my eyeballs. I could barely move, I had so many clothes on." She sniffed and reached for the scrap of material tucked into her sleeve. "It is particularly cold in this drawing room and it always is. I do not know why you insist on using it in the winter. It never fails that I catch a chill from spending too much time in here."

Lady Catherine pressed her lips together, choosing for the moment to ignore her impertinent daughter's words. She broke the seal on the missive and unfolded it, reading with creased brows.

When her mother lowered the note to her lap and looked off into space, Anne rolled her eyes again. "Are you going to share the contents of your express with me?"

Turning her now-focused gaze toward her child, the older woman's brows rose. "It is *my* express and therefore, *my* business. Who taught you to be so impudent? Was it Mrs. Jenkinson?" She moved her attention to Anne's companion, who was in a chair near the foot of her mistress' chaise, looking down at her clasped hands.

"No, it was not Mrs. Jenkinson, as you well know. Stop frightening her. Any impudence I have, I learned from you and from my cousins."

Lady Catherine frowned. "Yes, those boys are most assuredly impertinent. Perhaps I should have kept you separated from them more often." She sat in pensive silence for a heartbeat before she jumped a little, called back to her letter. "The express is from a Miss Caroline Bingley."

Anne rose up on one elbow. "Oh, I remember her. We met her in London before

Uncle Darcy passed away. She was still in school at that time. I remember wishing I could go, too."

"You were never healthy enough to go to a boarding school." Lady Catherine looked over the top of the paper she had lifted.

"I suppose not." Anne shrugged and snuggled back down under her blanket. "What did Miss Bingley have to say?"

Lady Catherine's brows creased again. "She says Darcy is in danger of forming an attachment to a completely inappropriate person who lives near the estate at which her party is staying."

At her cousin's name, Anne became instantly wary. "Oh?"

"Yes. She says she recalls me speaking to him about his duty and that she reminded him but sees no evidence that he listened to her advice. She writes that Miss Elizabeth Bennet is of low standing, with no fortune and an inappropriate family." Lady Catherine lowered the letter again. "Surely she cannot be serious. Darcy would never do something like that. He is engaged to you."

Anne shrunk even further down. "He has never asked."

Lady Catherine waved her hand as though to shoo away a fly that was bothering her. "He should not have to ask. His mother and I planned it when the pair of you were but babes."

"Mother, I have told you before that I do not want to marry Darcy."

"Nonsense! I have said it will be so, and therefore, you will obey. I am your mother and I know best." She rose from her chair. "I must go speak to him. I doubt it is true, but it behooves me to nip any gossip of this kind in the bud."

"But, Mama-"

"But nothing, Anne. You will marry him and that is the end of it. Mrs. Jenkinson, I think it wise for Miss de Bourgh to dine in her rooms tonight. I want her well-rested when my nephew comes and does his duty, which I am determined he will do immediately."

"Yes, madam." Mrs. Jenkinson stood and curtseyed, then carefully assisted Anne in rising. She escorted her silent charge out the door and up the stairs, shaking her head at the defeated posture of the normally confident young lady.

~~~***~~~

Lady Catherine was forced to delay her departure until morning, for as the butler pointed out when she called for the carriage, the night was dark and rainy, and the roads were dangerous, especially for a lady alone. At dawn the next day, she entered her equipage, a maid at her side, two grooms riding on the back of the barouche box, and one up with the driver. All were armed. Though she did not feel they needed to be, highwaymen did exist and she was not travelling her usual routes.

The ride was a long and uncomfortable one, but she finally arrived at Longbourn at about three o'clock. Her coachman had been required to ask for directions several times, first to Meryton, then to Longbourn. She was cold, tired, and filthy. All she really wanted was a hot bath and a bed, but she was on a mission. Luxuries could wait.

The coach came to a stop and Lady Catherine peeked outside to see a groom stride up the shallow steps to the porch. She let the curtain fall and tilted her head to try to hear.

"Excuse me, missus, but I am looking for Longbourn estate. Is this it?"

Lady Catherine could not hear the response from the servant who answered, but a minute or two later, the coach's door opened and the groom removed his hat and bowed.

"We have arrived, your ladyship." He stepped back at her nod, holding his hand out to assist her descent.

Lady Catherine allowed him to help her down, then shook out her skirts and squared her shoulders, taking in a deep breath. She let the air out through her nose and proceeded forward. She looked around at the clean and tidy steps and porch outside, and when invited to enter, inhaled the scent of beeswax.

She could see that the home was very well-maintained. A doubt about the veracity of Miss Bingley's letter niggled at the back of her mind, but Lady Catherine de Bourgh was not one to allow truth to get in the way of her desires, so she ignored it.

"Lady Catherine de Bourgh." The housekeeper introduced the guest and faded away as all good servants do, closing the door behind her.

Lady Catherine looked around her, taking in the faces of each of the ladies as they rose from their curtseys. She saw one open her mouth to speak – she supposed the mother, based on her age and cap – but cut the other woman off before she could form a single word. "Which of you is Miss Elizabeth Bennet?"

The six females glanced at each other. Without a word, one separated herself from the group, drawing herself up. "I am Elizabeth Bennet."

Lady Catherine pressed her lips together. She looked the girl up and down. "I would speak to you immediately."

Elizabeth's face cleared. She gestured behind her. "Please, do be seated. Shall I call for tea?"

"In private." Lady Catherine barked the words, striking the floor with her cane for emphasis. "There is a prettyish little wilderness out there. I am certain we would not be overheard in that area."

Now it was Elizabeth's turn to draw her lips into a thin line.

"Oh, Lizzy, do show her ladyship the gardens!" Mrs. Bennet waved the lace-trimmed bit of cloth in her hand toward the window. "Quickly, before she draws your father out of his bookroom. He is resting and must not be disturbed."

"Yes, Mama." Elizabeth turned from her mother to the visitor. "Please come with me." She skirted around the older woman and into the entry hall. Donning her pelisse, bonnet, and gloves, she smiled her thanks to the footman who opened the door and led her guest outside and into the gardens. She only stopped when Lady Catherine did.

"Do you know who I am?"

Elizabeth cocked a brow. "I am afraid I do not, your ladyship. I have never seen you in my life, nor have I heard of you."

"I am Lady Catherine de Bourgh, sister of the current Earl of Matlock."

Elizabeth blinked but remained silent.

"It is my understanding that you are acquainted with my nephew." Lady Catherine pounded her walking stick on the ground.

Now Elizabeth's brow creased. "And ... who is your nephew?"

Lady Catherine huffed in exasperation. "Do not pretend ignorance. I received a letter just yesterday telling me that you were trying to draw him in and make him forget his duty."

Shaking her head, Elizabeth did not try to hide the rolling of her eyes. "I am sorry, madam, but I know several gentlemen, though I have yet to attempt to 'draw in' a single one of them. You will have to be more specific in telling me which one is your nephew. Perhaps if you provided me with his name ..."

Again striking the dirt with her walking stick, Lady Catherine clarified. "Mr. Fitzwilliam Darcy of London and Pemberley in Derbyshire is my nephew."

Immediately, Elizabeth's brow smoothed. "Ah, I see. I am, indeed, acquainted with Mr. Darcy."

"And you have drawn him in with your arts and allurements. You have made him forget his duty to his family."

"I think not." Elizabeth bit her lip; Lady Catherine could see that it was an attempt to keep from laughing.

"What do you mean?"

"Madam, I have done nothing but avoid your nephew for most of his visit in the area."

"Are you saying you did not dance with him at a recent ball?" Lady Catherine was growing angry at Elizabeth's impertinence.

"I did; I have come to learn that he has an excellent character. He is not at all as I had initially thought him. So, when he requested the dances, I gave them to him." Elizabeth shrugged.

"Dances?" Lady Catherine emphasized the last letter in the word. "As in more than one set?" When Elizabeth confirmed it, she gasped. "My source was correct, then. Has my nephew made you an offer of marriage?"

Elizabeth choked and coughed, her hand over her mouth. She was silent for a moment, and then spoke. "I do not claim to be the most forthright of people; you may ask a question that I may choose not to answer. This would be one of those."

Lady Catherine was shocked into silence. "You are bound to have him, then? Did he tell you he is engaged to my daughter?"

Elizabeth paled but lifted her chin. "No, he did not. Why are you so concerned about him proposing to me if he is already betrothed? He does not strike me as dishonorable, and surely becoming engaged to two ladies at once is the definition of dishonorable."

It was Lady Catherine's turn to be uncomfortable. She swallowed and shifted her feet as her mind scrambled to form a response. "It is a peculiar engagement. His mother and I betrothed them when they were in their cradles. It was her greatest wish and mine for the estates of Rosings and Pemberley to be joined."

Elizabeth shrugged once again. "You did your part; it is now up to Mr. Darcy to fulfill it or not. It is not my doing if he chooses to marry elsewhere."

Lady Catherine clenched her jaw. "I ask you again: has my nephew made a proposal of marriage to you?"

Elizabeth was silent for a moment. When her answer came, it was quietly given. "He has not." Her eyes cast downward.

Lady Catherine closed her eyes in relief. "Do you promise to never enter into an engagement with him?"

Her gaze rising from her feet to look her antagonist directly in the eye, Elizabeth spoke clearly. "I will not."

With a gasp, Lady Catherine began to berate the younger woman, disparaging her person and her family.

Elizabeth stood for a few minutes in silence, though to the other lady, she did not appear to be listening. Eventually, she took advantage of a break in the flow of Lady Catherine's words to have her final say. "You have insulted me most grievously, and I must insist you leave at once." She turned on her heel and walked away, the older woman's invectives ringing in her ears.

Chapter 10

Elizabeth strode up the steps and into the entry hall, shutting the door firmly behind her. With choppy movements, she untied her bonnet and ripped her gloves off. She thrust the items at the housekeeper and untied the ribbons holding her pelisse together with shaking fingers. Having handed that garment over to Mrs. Hill, as well, she paused. She could hear her sisters and mother in the drawing room. No sound emanated from her father's book room. *I cannot disturb him, anyway*, she thought. Wishing for quiet and space to think, she hurried toward the staircase, only for her movements to be arrested by the sound of Mrs. Bennet calling her name. She slowly turned and trudged toward her.

"Where did your guest go? I was going to ask her to stay for tea." Mrs. Bennet stood at the window watching the grand carriage roll down the drive. "What happened?" She turned and peered at her second daughter.

"I do not know where she went. Perhaps to Netherfield." Elizabeth twisted her fingers together to hide their continued shaking.

"Who was she?" Mrs. Bennet returned to her favorite seat. "I have already ordered the tea. We will have to consume it ourselves. Come, sit down and tell us what she wanted."

The last thing Elizabeth wished was to tell her mother what Lady Catherine came to Longbourn for. However, she was not in the habit of disobeying a direct order, so she complied, taking a seat at the table with a small smile.

"She is Mr. Darcy's aunt. She somehow heard that we danced and came to make herself known to me." Elizabeth crossed her fingers in her lap, hiding them in the folds of her gown.

Mrs. Bennet's brows rose. "Really? I wonder why she would do such a thing?" She paused to pour a cup of tea. "Though, he did dance two sets with you. Perhaps he likes you."

Having no reply to that, Elizabeth remained silent.

"If she plans a long enough visit to Netherfield, we shall invite her to dine with us." Mrs. Bennet looked her daughter up and down with a critical eye. "We must impress upon her your suitability to be his wife and mistress of his homes. You must wear one of your better gowns. That one is old and out of style."

"Yes, Mama," Elizabeth murmured as she sipped her tea.

Eventually, though not soon enough to please Elizabeth, her mother had run through all the observations she could make and allowed her daughter to leave. This Elizabeth did, with as much haste as she could and still be thought a lady. Jane followed.

When they arrived at Elizabeth's room, Jane shut the door behind her. "What is the matter, Lizzy? I could see from your pallor that you did not wish to discuss Lady Catherine's visit." She perched on the edge of the bed and watched her younger sister pace the room.

"Oh, Jane." Elizabeth stopped and threw her hands in the air, before plopping down on the bed beside the other girl. She took a deep breath in through her nose, held it, then let it out. "She was here because she heard about my dances with her nephew and assumed that meant he proposed to me."

"Why did you not tell Mama that?" Jane's brow creased. "And, why would she assume such a thing? I believe he does like you a great deal, but it does not follow that he would propose. It was a small public assembly, not a private ball. There were more ladies than gentlemen, so it was no surprise to anyone that you danced twice with one person."

"I know. I do not know why she would make such assumptions." Elizabeth fell back onto the bed.

Jane turned and rested her knee on the mattress, to better see her sister's expressions. She tilted her head as she thought about Elizabeth's words and actions. "There is something you are not saying."

Elizabeth frowned and lifted her head. "Sometimes, being as close to one's sister as I am to you makes things uncomfortable, you know." She allowed her head to drop back down as Jane giggled.

"Come now; out with it. You will feel better having talked it out." Jane paused. "Do you wish it were true? Is that the problem?"

Elizabeth sighed and threw an arm over her eyes. "Yes, it is. When I first met Mr. Darcy, I thought him the handsomest gentlemen I had ever seen. Then, he behaved arrogantly, or so I thought, and I was disappointed. I began to avoid him as much as possible. But then, he spoke to Lydia and Kitty and their behavior improved. He did it again at Lucas Lodge. Then, he asked me to dance." She sighed again.

"And your opinion of him rose." Jane watched as Elizabeth nodded. "Do you want to know what I think?"

"Yes, I do." Elizabeth moved her arm and opened her eyes but remained prone.

"Charles and I have both noticed his attention to you and our sisters. Lydia and Kitty he clearly wished to warn. His interactions with them were different than those he had with you. He watches you constantly. Charles thinks he is developing an attachment to you. We have spoken about how nice it would be for the two of you to marry. We need never be far from each other, should that happen."

Elizabeth sat up. "Oh, Jane! I do not know if I should laugh or cry! Charlotte said the same last week, that Mr. Darcy looks at me. I would be beyond happy if he would fall in love with me, but he is so high above us socially. He is one of the wealthiest gentlemen in all of England. He could have anyone." She looked down as Lady Catherine's words rang in her memory. "His aunt says he is engaged to her daughter. If that is true, it does not matter how I feel, or how he feels."

Jane's brow creased. "She said *what*? That cannot be correct. Charles assured me his friend was not attached to anyone else."

Elizabeth looked up in surprise. "You *asked* him about it? Who are you and what have you done with my very proper sister?"

Jane blushed. "Charles is very easy to talk to. We are so similar, though he is far more gregarious than I. It just happens ..." Jane fluttered her hand as though to wave a fly away. "One moment, we are speaking of the weather and the next, we are sharing information about things we should not be talking about in the first place. I cannot help it." She looked up when Elizabeth laughed. "Oh, stop. You wait until you fall in love. Then, it will be my turn to laugh." She reached behind her to grab a pillow and hit her sister with it.

Elizabeth squealed when the pillow made contact with her arm. "Ouch!" She snatched it out of Jane's hand before the older girl could use it again. The pair laughed for a couple minutes, then quieted.

Jane held her sister's hand. "Lizzy, if Mr. Darcy did propose, would you accept?"

Elizabeth nodded. "Yes, I believe I would. He is everything I have wished for in a husband: kind, generous, and respectful. He never makes me feel as though my opinions do not matter, and he takes his responsibilities seriously. If I allowed myself, I could fall very deeply in love with him."

Jane smiled and squeezed the hand she held. "Then, we will have to hope he does."

After a moment of silence, Jane left Elizabeth to her thoughts.

Netherfield, a little while later

Though weary from her travels, Lady Catherine was still enraged by her visit to Longbourn. She spent the time it took to drive to Netherfield alternately berating Elizabeth and formulating her arguments with Darcy. She exited her carriage with great energy, charging up the steps to the open front door. She barrelled into the building, stopping when she noticed Miss Bingley standing near the door.

"Lady Catherine! How good of you to visit us!" Caroline dipped an elegant curtsey, lips lifted at the corners in a *ton*-approved smile.

Lady Catherine looked down her nose. "I need to speak to my nephew, immediately."

"I am sorry, but he is not here. He and my brothers were invited to a neighboring estate for a day of sport. I am uncertain when they plan to return. We had no idea you would arrive today, or I would have tried to keep Mr. Darcy here." Caroline paused. "Would you like to sit with me and my sister and have tea and something to eat? Or, would you prefer to retire? We have a room at the ready."

Lady Catherine pressed her lips together. "He is not here? How far away is this estate?"

"I believe my brother said it was ten miles on the other side of Meryton, my lady." Caroline watched her guest carefully.

With a creased brow and a frown, Lady Catherine considered her choices. She was tired, hungry, and filthy, and not looking forward to sitting in that coach for any further amount of time. She sighed internally. There was no help for it. She must spend the night. She intended to speak to her nephew at the earliest possible moment. "I will retire to this room you mentioned. I will take a tray." She flicked a distrustful glance at the open doorway of the drawing room where Louisa could be seen lounging on a sofa. "You will take me there immediately."

"Yes, your ladyship." Caroline gracefully indicated the staircase with her arm. "The suite is on the second floor." She then followed the older woman up.

A few minutes later, Caroline reentered the drawing room. She closed the door behind her and turned, biting down a smile. She drew in a deep breath and exhaled, then made her way to her sister's side, forcing herself to walk slowly.

Louisa looked up from admiring her rings and, seeing Caroline's demeanor, narrowed her eyes and frowned. "What are you up to? Who was that at the door?"

"That was Mr. Darcy's aunt, Lady Catherine de Bourgh. I have escorted her upstairs and to a chamber for the night. She wishes to speak to her nephew but, of course, he is not here." Caroline gracefully perched on a chair.

Louisa was silent as she thought about the sudden appearance of their guest's relative. "You have been behaving strangely all day." She accompanied her observation with a quirked brow. "You knew she was coming, did you not? Did you do something to bring her here? How is it that you had a room ready in so short a time? You never brought her into this one. She has not been here a quarter hour."

Caroline lifted the corners of her lips. She looked down and began fidgeting with her bracelets. "As a matter of fact, I sent her an express yesterday. I had hoped she would come, and she has."

Louisa's eyes grew wide. "Why would you do that?"

Caroline sniffed. "Because Mr. Darcy is making eyes at a totally unsuitable young lady. He will not listen to me about his duty, so I called upon the one person I thought he might obey."

Shaking her head, Louisa closed her mouth, which had fallen open at her sister's explanation. "Really? I do not know where to begin with this one. I am uncertain our brother's friend will appreciate you meddling in his business."

"He must see that I am his perfect match. I will do whatever it takes to open his eyes to that fact." Caroline dropped all pretense at cordiality, instead snapping at Louisa.

In silence, the other lady looked at her, jaw clenched and lips pressed together. She stood. "Let us hope it all works out in a way that pleases you. I think I will retire now. Good night."

Caroline watched her sister leave the room with narrowed eyes. She shrugged before a triumphant smile twisted her lips. "Oh, it will, I assure you." She followed Louisa up, but was unable to sleep. Excitement kept her awake long into the night.

Chapter 11

Hours later, three bleary-eyed gentlemen made their way from Netherfield's stables to its house. Darcy and Hurst were on either side of an unsteady Bingley, keeping him from falling over as he enthusiastically sang.

"Leave it to you, Bingley, to become even more like yourself when inebriated." Darcy's observation drew a laugh from his companions. "Anyone else would behave in a manner completely opposite of their usual habits."

"I am just a happy fellow." Bingley grinned and lurched toward his friend. "You do the same, you know. The more you drink, the ... oops, sorry, Hurst ... the quieter you become."

Hurst pushed his brother-in-law upright again. "He is correct, you know, Darcy. You do become quieter, and your wit sharper. You are more likely to let it loose after a few drinks, though, than is your usual wont."

"Hmph." Darcy grunted but said nothing else until they were nearly to the house. "I suppose you are correct. Thankfully, I rarely drink to excess. I am glad I remained reasonably sober tonight. Only Bingley would be swayed to visit a tavern after a day of fox hunting."

Hurst laughed. "You have to admit, that Goulding boy was rather persuasive. He clearly enjoys his time with that serving girl."

"Yes," Darcy replied dryly. He rolled his eyes. "I wonder if his father knows."

"Oh, no doubt he does. As long as he does not propose marriage to the girl, I would imagine his parents will not care."

Darcy had nothing to say to that and so remained silent. He did not understand the propensity of the gentry to behave in such a manner. He did not. His father had warned him of the dangers of such behavior and had given strict instructions on how Darcy was to behave, rules he followed to this day. It was often difficult, but he was happy that he had the self-control to avoid disease and illegitimate children.

Between Darcy and Hurst, they got Bingley in the house and to his rooms. Each went to his own suite then, eager to sleep off the effects of the long day. Darcy's valet met him in his dressing room.

"Lady Catherine de Bourgh arrived this evening, sir."

"What?" Darcy's jaw dropped. "How did she know where I was? I assume she has been given a room. Do you know what she wants? Good heavens, she is everywhere." Darcy wrinkled his nose and shook his head.

Smith cleared his throat. "I have been told the only thing she said was that she wished to speak to you. Miss Bingley had ordered a room prepared for visitors earlier in the day; one can only assume she knew the lady was coming."

"If I were a betting man, I would say Miss Bingley is the entire reason for my aunt's visit." Darcy shook his head and rolled his eyes. He began to remove his coat before he continued to speak. "She is somewhere in the house, then?"

"Yes, sir. On this floor in the other wing." Smith untied Darcy's cravat and slid it off his neck.

"At least she is not next door." Darcy's muttered words were accompanied by the clink of his cufflinks hitting the marble top of the dresser. He undressed in silence, considering this unexpected turn of events and what his aunt could possibly be after. Donning his nightshirt, he spoke once more. "Undoubtedly, she will be up with the crows and desire an audience with me. I am going to bed; I will need as much sleep as I can get to deal with her. Please wait to wake me until she makes the request."

"As you wish." Smith bowed and turned to put his master's clothes away as Darcy wandered into the other room.

Climbing up into the large bed, Darcy reclined, pulling the covers over himself. He fell instantly asleep, concerns about his aunt's presence fading into the back of his mind.

Thankfully for Darcy, Lady Catherine did not rise with the dawn to confront him. Her weariness had been so great that she slept far into the morning, and he was able to face her reasonably well-rested and with a sharp mind. He had descended the stairs to break his fast when Smith found him.

"Lady Catherine has requested to see you at ten o'clock, sir."

Darcy pressed his lips together, suppressing an urge to roll his eyes. "Very well." He glanced at the clock above the fireplace. "I will meet her in the library at ten. That gives me enough time to break my fast. Have tea and coffee set up in there, in case my aunt requires it."

With a bow, Smith turned sharply and exited the room, intent on completing his employer's instructions.

Darcy ate his breakfast, enjoying the quiet. Bingley would likely not be seen before noon, and his sisters never came down before then, so he took full advantage of it. Finally, though, the time of his meeting with his mother's sister arrived. With a sigh, he set the now-empty coffee cup on the table and stood, brushing crumbs off his clothing. He was not surprised to arrive in the library to find his aunt was not there. He paced the room, examining the knick-knacks that were placed on the poorly-stocked bookshelves. He heard Lady Catherine's walking stick before he saw her. He turned and waited, erect and calm, for her entrance.

"There you are, Nephew." She tapped her stick on the floor, both hands on the head. The thick carpet softened the sound to a dull thud.

Darcy bowed. "Indeed. Welcome to Netherfield, Aunt." He gestured to a set of chairs and a small table, where the coffee and tea service had been placed a few moments before. "Shall we sit down?" After he assisted the elderly lady into a chair, he sat in the one next to it. "I was told you wished to speak to me."

"I do." Lady Catherine launched directly into her speech without giving Darcy an opening to respond. "Though I know it must be a gross falsehood, I was told that you were forming an attachment to a local lady and had ignored reminders about your duty. I immediately traveled to this place to discover for myself the veracity of the matter. I have thought about it all night, and despite what was implied to me yesterday, I know you would never propose marriage to someone unsuitable, though that impertinent chit refused to assure me she would refuse you if you *did* offer for her."

Darcy had immediately recognized that his aunt was going to try to run roughshod over him. He sat back, legs crossed with his hands clasped over one knee, and let her speak. It was only when he heard the words "impertinent chit" that he sat up, surprised, and sought to interrupt. "Excuse me, Aunt. Of whom are you speaking?"

Lady Catherine's mouth hung open for a second, so shocked was she to be interrupted. "Why, that girl, from that estate. Miss Elizabeth Bennet."

Darcy took a deep breath, willing himself to calm. "Are you telling me you went to Longbourn and spoke to Miss Elizabeth without an introduction?" He closed his eyes for a moment as dread filled his heart.

"I did. Why should I not? I am the sister of an earl. I need no introductions to do what I need to do. She is a threat to my Anne. I will not have her thinking she can expect your addresses."

"I have told you once before that I will not marry my cousin. She and I have spoken of it and neither of us wish it." Darcy stood and began to pace. "I should have been more forceful about it, and then you would not still be carrying on with the idea." He stopped and turned towards her. "I apologize. I have let you go on speaking of an engagement between us because I wished to show respect. Instead of correcting you, I have allowed you to continue in a fantasy that will never come to fruition. I am ashamed that I have behaved in so ungentlemanly a fashion. Do forgive me." He sketched a quick bow and straightened, waiting for his aunt's response.

"Fantasy? It is no fantasy! Your mother and I betrothed the pair of you when you were babies. You are engaged to Anne!" Lady Catherine surged to her feet.

Darcy breathed in deep before he replied. "No, she did not. She spoke of it as a good idea, something she wished for, but only if it made me happy. It does not do so, and therefore, I am not bound by her desires." He held a hand up to stop his aunt when she opened her mouth. "There was no formal engagement, Aunt. No marriage articles were signed. My father would not have allowed it; he told me so himself. Despite what you seem to think is correct, neither of my parents believed me to be engaged to my cousin. I will marry where I wish and nowhere else."

Lady Catherine clenched her jaw as she listened. When Darcy stopped speaking, she took up her arguments again. "Are you determined to have the chit, then? Rest assured that unless you marry my daughter, you will be dead to me. You have a duty to marry well. Anne comes from the finest bloodlines. Her grandfather was an earl; her uncle is an earl. We have ties to royalty. She is your perfect match. That Bennet girl has nothing but her arts and allurements to tempt you. I left her under no illusions about my opinion of her and her grasping family. Now I do the same to you." After repeating to her nephew some of the things she had said to Elizabeth, she reminded him of her threat. "I am leaving this place now." She looked Darcy in the eye. "You will think about all I have said. I know you will make the correct decision. I expect you at Rosings within the week." She turned on her heel and sailed out of the library, chin held high.

Darcy graced his retreating aunt with a shallow bow that she did not see. He remained rooted in place for a long moment, muscles rigid and teeth clenched. Anger at her presumption warred with embarrassment that she would presume to not only order his life for him, but to confront a total stranger. When he was certain he had his emotions under enough control that he would not lash out, he moved, striding first to the door to shut and lock it, then pacing the perimeter of the room.

"Who does she think she is?" He snorted. "She *thinks* she is the head of my family. She can think again. She is not my mother. Even Mama would not get far with me, behaving in such a fashion." Darcy shook his head and glared at the globe resting on the nearly-empty shelf that sat head-high in the corner of the room. "I will not be directed. I am the head of my family and I will be respected."

Having vented his spleen, he fell silent, though he continued his pacing. He mentally reviewed the confrontation, reliving every piece of the argument. Eventually, his pacing slowed and then stopped. He dropped into a wingback chair in front of the fireplace, feeling the warmth of the blaze wash over him. He rested his head against the back and closed his eyes. "She spoke to Elizabeth, and in such a manner! How can I ever face her again? Those fine eyes will be filled with pain and distrust." He groaned at the image that filled his mind, lifting his hands to run them over his face and hair. "Should I apologize? I should." He gripped his hair and pulled, frustration propelling him up and out of his seat. "No, I should not. It may cause more pain to do so. Did I not decide I could not offer for her? My aunt was correct about Elizabeth's connections and standing. I cannot deny that." He groaned again and took two steps toward the fire, leaning his arm on the mantel and his head on his arm. "What a mess."

Darcy remained locked in the library for several hours, agonizing over the events of the morning and wishing he could simply throw over his duty and ride to Longbourn to propose to the woman he knew he loved.

Chapter 12

Caroline waited in vain for Lady Catherine to come downstairs and break her fast. When she heard the elderly lady descend, she patted her hair and shook out her skirts to assure herself that she was presentable. Unfortunately, the tap of the lady's cane told the story ... Lady Catherine had skipped breakfast. Caroline pulled aside a footman and hissed a question at him.

"Where is Lady Catherine going?"

The footman bowed. "I was told she wished to speak to her nephew. I just now delivered a tray with tea and coffee on it. Mr. Darcy was in the room waiting for her."

"What room?" Caroline shook his arm.

The servant's mien remained impassive, though red began to creep up his neck. His tone was cold when he spoke. "The library."

Caroline did not notice the footman's reaction to her abuse. She dismissed him, oblivious to the glare he threw over his shoulder at her as he passed through the servant's entrance.

With a quick look around, Caroline realized that she was the only occupant of the room. She slipped out the door, relieved to not have to come up with an excuse to do so. She paused in the hall, tapping her lip with her finger. She eyed the library door for a moment, then moved her gaze down the hall. When they fell onto the door to the back stairs, her eyes lit up.

Caroline had spent some time the first few days of her residence at Netherfield looking for entrances to the rooms. She knew the back stairs were in a small room that had two doors in it, one leading to her brother's study and one to the library. Further, she knew that this back door of the library opened into a small room that could be used for study or quiet reading. She would be able to hear everything Darcy and his aunt said by simply opening just a tiny bit the door between the antechamber and the library proper.

Caroline tiptoed across the tiny chamber and slowly opened the door a crack. She pulled a chair across the carpeted space and placed it near the door but out of sight of anyone who should walk by in the larger room. Then, she settled in to listen.

She heard with glee the things Lady Catherine reported to Darcy that she had said to Elizabeth Bennet. Her delight dimmed at hearing of the elder lady's desire for him to marry his cousin, but when he said he would not, Caroline grinned and settled back in her chair. When she heard Lady Catherine exit the room, she cocked her head to listen intently, but could not determine if Darcy had left with his aunt or not. Just as she was about to stand and peek into the library, she heard him begin to mutter.

Try as she might, Caroline could not make out what Darcy said, as he kept his tone of voice low. She tried to wait him out, but it soon became clear that he intended to remain within for the time being, so she reluctantly rose and stealthily made her way up the servant's stairs to her bedchamber.

Once locked inside her rooms, Caroline began to pace back and forth as she considered what she had overheard. "He is not going to marry his cousin, of that I am assured," she said to herself. She wrapped one arm around her torso and tapped her lip with one of the fingers of her other hand. "This is good, but he did not say he would not marry Eliza Bennet. I cannot trust him to depart from here and leave her behind. I must take action if I want to be the next Mrs. Darcy." After thinking a bit longer, she hit upon the perfect plan.

Caroline kept a sharp eye out the rest of the day for an opportunity to implement her plan. It was nearly dinner time before Darcy emerged from the library and requested his horse be saddled and held at the stables. She smiled before hurrying out through the glass doors of the drawing room, across the veranda, and into the gardens. Picking up her skirts, she raced through the manicured yard and across the drive to the stables. She paused at the open double doors to catch her breath, fanning her face with one hand while she pressed the other to her chest. She could hear the grooms at work inside, talking to each other, as well as to the horses. She peeked into the building and, not seeing anyone, tiptoed in. She found an empty stall and slipped through the portal. Looking around with a grimace at the dusty room with its hay-covered floor, she shuddered and then lifted her skirts, ducking behind the front wall.

Crouching so she could not be seen, Caroline listened to the activity in the barn. She heard a horse being walked into the center aisle while a groom spoke softly to it. She listened as the young man grunted with the effort of tossing the saddle up onto the animal's back. Then, she leaned against the side of the stall, going over her plan in her mind. Finally, she heard Darcy's deep voice as he entered the building. Now was the time.

Caroline threw herself down into the hay. She arranged herself into what she imagined was an enticing position. Then, she cried out.

"Mr. Darcy! Is that you?"

The men in the aisle stopped all movement and speaking. Caroline waited for a moment. "Mr. Darcy! In here!"

A moment later, her prey was at the stall door. "Miss Bingley!" He rushed in. "What happened?"

Caroline smiled up at him, batting her eyelashes. "Why, nothing. I was waiting for you. Did we not arrange to meet here?" She glanced over Darcy's shoulder, making sure at least one groom heard her words.

"What are you speaking of? I made no assignation with you." Darcy shook his head. "Get up, Miss Bingley. I am certain your brother would like to hear about this from your mouth, not just mine."

Caroline's eyes widened as she pressed a hand to her chest. "Oh, but you did!" Glancing behind him again, she noted the additional servants that had gathered. With a sly look, she gestured to Darcy. "Please do help me up." Darcy made to oblige her, but when he leaned over and extended his hand, she reached up and tore her gown at the shoulder. "Mr. Darcy!" Her cry, along with the sound of tearing cloth, made the grooms gasp.

Darcy stiffened. He straightened and stepped back, then turned. "I believe Mr. Bingley is at Longbourn," he said to the gathered staff. "Send someone to fetch him. Immediately." He paused. "You there, bring me a blanket from the tack room. Miss Bingley has need of it. The rest of you, return to your duties. Apollo must be unsaddled and moved back into his stall." He sighed. "I will not have time for a ride, now." When the staff had all moved away and the groom returned with a saddle blanket, Darcy accepted the woolen rectangle and dismissed him. Then, he turned to his friend's sister.

"Cover yourself." He tossed the blanket to her.

"You must marry me. I have been compromised in front of witnesses." Caroline arranged the smelly item around her shoulders.

Darcy rolled his eyes. When he spoke, his words were clipped. "I do not have to marry you. Were this incident to reach the ears of the *ton*, and I am quite certain it eventually will, blame for your supposed ruin will be laid firmly where it belongs – at your feet. You are well aware that the woman is always blamed for such things while gentlemen are free to go about their lives as they always have."

Caroline struggled to rise from the floor. "But ... you are a gentleman of honor! Of course you will marry me! Your honor will insist upon it." Finally on her feet, she crossed her arms and lifted her chin. "Charles will force you, if you choose not to do the right thing."

Darcy snorted. "No, he will not. He has been told multiple times that I would never marry you, under any circumstances."

Caroline began to protest, but Darcy turned his back and ignored her, and she eventually stopped, instead clenching her jaw and narrowing her eyes at his back. "Well," she huffed, "I have no intentions of waiting around in the stables for my brother to return. I will be in my chambers." She pushed her way past Darcy and stomped back toward the house.

Darcy shook his head. He ground his teeth together, hoping to keep the words whirling around in his brain from spilling out. *As if I would marry her,* he thought.

"A right bold one, that Miss Bingley." The stable master, a gray-haired, whip-thin man with a weathered countenance named Bernard Sampford, leaned against the other side of the stall door. "I have served here for forty years, in one capacity or another, and I have to say she's about the boldest I have seen." He paused, tilting his head to look Darcy up and down. "You did the right thing there, I think. She would make you miserable."

Darcy had stiffened when Sampford began to speak so familiarly to him. However, he could not fault the man's powers of observation, which led him to unbend enough to speak about Caroline's incredible compromise attempt. "That she would, but do not tell her or my friend I said it."

Sampford chuckled. "I know nothing, sir. I have lasted as long as I have here by knowing when to keep my mouth shut and when to open it." He winked.

Darcy chuckled as he watched the stable master shuffle away. He shook his head, his lips continuing to twitch, until his brain reminded him of what his life could have been, had the events of the evening played out differently. He shuddered as scenes of his life as the husband of Caroline Bingley played out in his mind. His stomach clenched, forcing him into motion. He stepped out of the stable to pace in front of the doors on the driveway. He was so deep into his contemplations, imagining all manner of misery, that he did not see his friend approaching.

"Darcy!" Bingley leaped off his gelding, tossing the reins to a nearby groom. "What has happened?"

Darcy jumped, startled, at the sound of the other gentleman's voice. "I did not hear you ride up."

Bingley chuckled. "I apologize for frightening you." He winked when his friend rolled his eyes. "Toby said something about my sister and a stall."

Darcy's lips pressed together for a moment while he formed the words to tell Bingley what happened. "She tried to compromise me." When the other man groaned and threw his head back, Darcy continued. "I have told you for years I would not marry her."

Bingley looked Darcy in the eye. "I know that, and I have told her that, repeatedly." He shook his head. "Who saw her?"

Darcy shrugged. "I do not know. A couple of the grooms, at least. Toby, for certain. The boy who fetched the saddle blanket to cover her probably either saw or has figured it out."

"She needed a saddle blanket to cover her." Bingley's tone was flat. "Tell me she did not rip her clothing on purpose."

"I wish I could." Darcy winced as his friend's shoulders drooped.

Bingley sighed deeply. "Very well, then. Let us go to the house and confront her."

The pair made their way from the stables to the front door in silent contemplation. As they reached the steps leading into the house, Bingley laid his hand on Darcy's arm, stopping them both.

"I apologize. No matter what my sister says or does, you can be assured that she will face the consequences on her own. I will not have her here while you remain."

"Where will you send her?"

Bingley shrugged. "Probably to London. She had a suitor of sorts in the spring. I will see if he is still interested."

"She may refuse him, even yet."

Bingley cocked his head, his gaze sliding away. "She probably will." He looked back at Darcy. "However, she has compromised herself. You and I both know the stable staff will not keep her actions to themselves, and we both also know it will not remain here in this area. Stories like hers are too delicious in the mouths of gossipers. It will travel, and be passed from servants to gentry. Once there, it will spread like wildfire, including to town. Her reputation is as good as ruined already. If she is to have any hope of marrying, it must be done quickly."

Darcy nodded. "You are likely correct." He paused. "What was her objection to her suitor? Who was he?"

"Lord Hubert Blackwell. He is a baron from Warwickshire. From what I gather, he was too dictatorial." Bingley snorted. "Caroline, as you know, does not like to be told what to do. One would think she had read Wollenstonecraft and was a devoted follower, the way she insists on always having her own way."

Darcy chuckled. "Indeed. Are you certain she has not?"

Bingley looked at his friend as though Darcy had grown a second head. "Caroline? Read? Are you joking?"

Darcy laughed. "Point taken." He clapped his hand on his friend's shoulder. "Come on. Let us beard the dragon."

With a deep sigh, Bingley turned and followed Darcy into the house.

Once within, the gentlemen handed their hats, gloves, and greatcoats to the housekeeper.

"Where might I find my family?"

Mrs. Nichols looked down. "Miss Bingley has retired to her rooms. I understand Mrs. Hurst has followed. Miss Bingley seemed insistent upon her sister's company. I believe Mr. Hurst is in the billiards room."

Seeing Bingley hesitate, Darcy inquired, "Did Miss Bingley give a reason for retiring so early?"

The housekeeper cleared her throat, glanced up at her employer, then dropped her gaze again. "I could not make out everything she was saying; she was crying and screaming. It was ..." she glanced up again, this time briefly meeting Darcy's eyes. "Quite a scene."

Bingley groaned. Darcy merely nodded. "That will be all, I think." He looked at his friend. "Bingley?"

"Yes, that will be all. Thank you, Mrs. Nichols."

The housekeeper curtseyed and hurried away.

Chapter 13

"We should check with Hurst first. He probably heard it all." Bingley turned toward the back of the house, Darcy following closely behind.

Hurst stood from where he had been leaning over the billiards table when his brother-in-law and Darcy entered the game room. "A fine kettle of fish we seem to have gotten ourselves into." He gazed intently at Darcy. "Are you well?"

Darcy nodded as he dropped into one of the room's chairs. "I am."

Bingley interrupted. "What has she said?"

Hurst shrugged as he laid his stick on the table. "Something about Darcy and an assignation and being caught in the act."

Darcy huffed and looked toward the blazing fire to his right. He was silent for a moment as he brought his emotions under control. When he thought he could speak calmly, he did. "She was, indeed, 'caught in the act,' but not the act she seems to have implied to you."

"I thought as much." Hurst leaned back and linked his fingers over his stomach. "What did happen?"

"She was waiting in an empty stall when I arrived, on the floor in the dirt. When I reached down to assist her in rising, she ripped her gown."

Hurst shook his head. He accepted the tumbler of port Bingley offered him. "She set you up. Are you going to marry her?"

"No." Darcy's refusal was unequivocal. "I have told Bingley this."

Hurst nodded. "As much as I would enjoy being your brother, and as dearly as I would love Caroline to marry high and live elsewhere, I do not blame you for refusing. She would make you miserable."

"That is exactly what I said." Bingley had taken possession of the third chair in the grouping and now put his feet up on the small, marble-topped table in the middle of the arrangement. "I want to send her to London, but I also need a hostess for the ball at the end of the week."

"Louisa and I can escort her to town tomorrow and return for the ball. I assume the planning is complete at this point. Mrs. Nichols can send word via express if she has questions. Caroline is not needed at all at this point." Hurst took a sip of his port. "Today is, what, Monday? We can be in London tomorrow afternoon, rest on Wednesday, and return in time for dinner on Thursday."

"Who will she stay with in town?" Darcy tilted his head as his gaze moved between

Hurst and Bingley. "Will she not need a companion of some sort?"

"Probably." Bingley frowned as he stared into the fire. "She is not without friends. Surely one would be willing to spend a few days with her, or even a few weeks."

"Given Caroline's propensity for doing what she wishes, we should invite the lady to stay at your townhouse, with your sister, rather than Caroline going to her friend." Hurst waited for Bingley to acknowledge his words before he spoke again. "She and Miss Carter seemed to be close before we came here to Netherfield."

"Yes, they have been great friends for several years now. I am certain she is in town; I heard Caroline telling Louisa about it the other day." Bingley sipped his drink. "Miss Carter has an older woman as her companion. An aunt, I believe, whose husband died and left her in reduced circumstances. It would be the perfect situation."

Hurst nodded. "Good. I will have Louisa call on her on Wednesday, or perhaps send a note around."

Darcy observed the interactions between his friends. "It seems you have a plan in place, then." He stood. "I would like to retire. Will you have a tray sent up to my room?"

Bingley and Hurst rose, as well.

"I will do that right away." Bingley glanced at the clock. "I am certain the cook is upset; dinner is greatly delayed." He paused. "I will probably ask for a tray, as well, if I am even inclined to eat after talking with Caroline."

"Send a pair of them up to my chambers, then. I have no wish to dine alone at that large table, and Louisa will need something to eat, as well. She is unlikely to be willing to be so far from her sister tonight, I suspect." Hurst gestured toward the door. "Shall we?"

Darcy left the other gentlemen and ascended the staircase to his suite of rooms. He heard Caroline's raised voice drifting down the hallway, so he quickly ducked into his bedchamber, firmly closing the door behind him and locking it. Peeking into the dressing room and not spotting Smith, he rang the bell and began to pace the room, pulling at the knots in his cravat.

A short while later, after changing into his nightwear and consuming the meal Smith brought up for him, Darcy settled into bed. The thoughts, memories, and emotions he had tried to suppress all evening assailed him as he lay in the quiet darkness. For a long time, he tossed and turned, but he eventually fell into an exhausted sleep.

The next morning, Darcy rose just after dawn, bleary-eyed and feeling as though he had been run over by a carriage. His sleep had been restless, filled with dreams – nightmares, really – of being married first to his cousin, then to Caroline, and finally to some nameless heiress from the first circles. He sat on the edge of the bed for a long time, head resting in his hands, as the misery he had experienced in his night time wanderings washed over him.

"I cannot do it." Darcy gripped his hair as his fists clenched. "Duty has been pounded into me for as long as I can remember, but I cannot do it." Taking a deep breath, he stood and walked to the window nearest the bed. He leaned on the frame and looked out at the chilly morning. He closed his eyes, seeing Elizabeth's sparkling orbs and saucy smile. The pain in his heart eased as he thought of her and he knew she was the answer. He knew what he must do.

~~~***~~~

As soon as it was a decent time to do so, Darcy ordered Apollo saddled and headed toward Longbourn. As he rode, he practiced what and how he would say the words he knew needed to be said.

Darcy crossed the property line between Netherfield and Longbourn deep in thought. A flash of white in the woods alongside the road caught his attention. He pulled his horse to a stop and peered into the trees. "Miss Elizabeth!"

Darcy waited until Elizabeth had spun toward him to dismount. He led Apollo into

139

the wood line until he was directly in front of the woman he loved.

"Good morning." Elizabeth curtseyed. "I hope you are well."

Darcy stared for a long moment, spell-bound as always in her presence. "I am." He glanced down to see that he was playing with the reins. Gripping the lengths of leather, he tucked his hands behind his back. "I was coming to your house, to see you. I need to speak with you."

Elizabeth's gaze wandered over Darcy's face. She tilted her head. "We are here to-gether now." She looked around. "There are two or three tree stumps just over there." She gestured down the path and looked back at him. "Perhaps we can speak here? Or do you need to wait until I get back to Longbourn?"

"Oh. No, here is good." Darcy held his elbow out to her. "Please; lead the way."

When they arrived at the spot where a bunch of trees had been felled in a previous year, Darcy assisted Elizabeth in sitting on one of the stumps. He then took a place on another for a brief moment before jumping up to pace before her. After a few minutes of gathering his courage, he stopped in front of her, took a deep breath, and forced the words out of his mouth.

"Allow me to apologize to you for the distress my aunt caused you and your household. I know she must have upset you;

she told me what she said and it was upsetting to me. I can only imagine the depth of your feelings." He reluctantly lifted his gaze from Elizabeth's hands, clasped together in her lap, to her eyes. He did not wish to see the censure he was certain would be there, but knew he must.

Once his gaze connected with Elizabeth's, she smiled. "I accept your apology, though you are certainly not required to give one. That should be the employment of your aunt. It was she who gave the offense. You are blameless."

Relief swept through him. "Thank you," he whispered, closing his eyes. When he opened them again, Darcy centered them on Elizabeth's. "I would have you know that I am not now, nor have I ever been, betrothed to my cousin. That has been Lady Catherine's wish for many years, but neither my cousin nor I have any desire to wed each other."

A look he could not decipher passed over Elizabeth's countenance. "You are not?"

Darcy shook his head. "No, I am not. My heart is not Anne's and never will be. It belongs to another."

Elizabeth seemed to draw herself up. "Oh."

Darcy sank to his knees in the dirt before her. He grasped her hands in his. He stared deep into her eyes. "My heart belongs to you, Miss Elizabeth. From the first moment I laid my eyes on you, I wished to know more of you. I have been foolish these past weeks, thinking my duty mattered more than my growing feelings. However, the events of the past four and twenty hours have opened my eyes to my folly, and now I wish to declare myself and to ask if it would be possible for you to forgive me for the delay and consent to be my wife."

Elizabeth was quiet for a long moment, and Darcy could see the tears filling her eyes. He worried for a second or two, but then realized that, instead of pulling her hands from his, she was squeezing them tightly.

"I will marry you!" Elizabeth made a sound, half sob and half laugh. "I love you. I was so disappointed by your aunt's information. I have admired you from the beginning. I thought you did not like me." She stopped rambling when Darcy pulled her up and into his arms.

"Dearest Elizabeth. How could I do anything but love one as lively and kind as you?" Bending his head, he brushed his lips across hers. "Thank you. I love you."

Elizabeth's answering declaration was swallowed up by Darcy's kiss.

~~~***~~~

The next step for the newly engaged couple was for Darcy to ask for Mr. Bennet's permission. This he did, while Elizabeth assured her mother that Bennet's heart would be well and that Darcy would not be taxing it beyond what it could bear. When she was summoned to the book room, Elizabeth ignored Mrs. Bennet's protestations and happily scurried across the hall and down two doors, knocking on the portal to her father's domain.

"Come."

Elizabeth peeked inside before she stepped in and closed the wooden panel behind her. She smiled at Darcy and then turned her bright eyes toward her father.

"Come closer, my dear. It seems you have been busy this morning." Mr. Bennet winked at his favorite daughter.

Elizabeth blushed but smiled. "I have." She turned her adoring gaze up at Darcy, quickly losing herself in his answering stare.

Bennet cleared his throat. He waited a moment, then shook his head with a roll of his eyes and a smirk. "Elizabeth. Elizabeth!"

Both Elizabeth and Darcy jumped. They blushed and looked at the master of Longbourn.

"Have a seat, both of you." When the couple had obeyed, Bennet spoke again. "Mr. Darcy has requested permission to marry you, Lizzy, and has assured me that you have granted him your hand."

"I have. I have long wished for his good opinion, but feared I would never receive it in the manner I longed for. I love him, Papa."

Bennet nodded. "I can see that. I will admit that I noticed his attention to you on his previous visits. I had hoped a match would be made, but you avoided him for so long that I was doubtful."

Elizabeth's blush deepened. She glanced quickly at Darcy and then away again, down at her hands. "I thought he did not like me, and since I had no wish be left with a broken heart when he departed, I did my best to stay away from him." She looked at Darcy. "I am sorry."

"All is well, my love." Darcy took Elizabeth's hand and brought it to his lips. When he set it down again, he did not relinquish his hold.

Bennet leaned back in his chair with a sigh. "I must say, I am relieved at this outcome. I would wish all my girls married before I shuffle off this mortal coil, but I will be happy with two of you for now."

Someone knocked on the door just then, and Bennet called them in. it was Mrs. Hill with a tea tray. When she had set it on the table near the master's desk, she curtseyed and left the room.

Elizabeth moved to the table and began pouring without waiting for her father to ask. She handed out cups to the gentlemen, then plates with some of the small cakes on them that were part of the tea service. Then, she served herself and resumed her place beside Darcy.

"If I were you," Bennet began after taking a sip of tea, "I would not say anything to your mother just yet. She will persist in trying to discover what we have spoken of, but if you hold out, you may announce your engagement at the ball Mr. Bingley is hosting on Friday. Mrs. Bennet will gain far more pleasure out of a grand announcement, I think, than a simple one in our home."

Elizabeth smirked. "And it will save you having to listen to her exclamations, I suspect."

Bennet laughed. "You know me too well, Daughter."

When the trio emerged from the book room, Mrs. Bennet behaved just as expected. To her chagrin, none of them would appease her curiosity. She did eye Darcy suspiciously, however, when he stayed to visit as long as Bingley did.

Three days later, Darcy stood with Elizabeth at his side as Bingley stepped up onto the orchestra platform at the beginning of his ball and asked for everyone's attention.

"Thank you for coming out tonight. As you know, I am betrothed to the beautiful Miss Jane Bennet, and have been for the past year and some months. This ball was intended to be a celebration of our engagement and our upcoming wedding, but it has turned out to be much more. My friend, Darcy, has an announcement of his own to make." Bingley gestured for the other gentleman to step up beside him.

Darcy did as he was bid. He was uncomfortable being the center of attention and found himself fidgeting. Stiffening his spine, he lifted his chin, took a deep breath, and exhaled. "I am pleased to announce that Miss Elizabeth Bennet has granted me the honor of her hand. We will marry along with my friend Bingley and Miss Bennet on the third of December."

Mrs. Bennet's shriek was almost drowned out by the applause of her neighbors and Bingley's friends.

Chapter 14

The next day, Darcy and Elizabeth sat next to each other in front of the fire, casting adoring glances at each other. Bingley and Jane were on the other side of the fireplace doing the same, and Mrs. Bennet and her remaining daughters were employed in individual pursuits across the room.

Darcy watched as his beloved looked away, suddenly seeming uncomfortable. "Is something the matter, my love?" He itched to take her hand but could not in public as they were.

Elizabeth's shoulder lifted and fell. Her mouth opened and closed. Then, she straightened her spine and faced him fully. "I received a letter from your aunt in today's post."

Dread filled Darcy. "I am sorry. She sent me one, too." He paused before proceeding with a cautious tone to his voice. "What did she say?"

Elizabeth hesitated. She pulled the missive out of her pocket and handed it to him. "I would rather not speak of it. You may read it for yourself."

With his brow creased, Darcy did as he was bid, unfolding the note and starting to read. The further down the page his eyes travelled, the more stern his countenance became. He clenched his jaw as he folded the piece of paper once more and stood, his teeth grinding. He looked down at his betrothed. "Please forgive me, Elizabeth, for the suffering imposed upon you, both by Lady Catherine and by my next action." He stepped toward the fire, crumpled the letter in his hand, and tossed it into the blaze, where it briefly flared before being consumed by the flames.

Elizabeth said nothing, simply staring at Darcy as he resumed his place beside her.

Darcy glanced over his shoulder and, seeing the rest of the family engrossed in their tasks, reached for Elizabeth's hand. "I am sorry. I promise I will not make a habit of destroying your correspondence. However, there is no need for either of us to have to remember her vitriol in the future." He squeezed her fingers in his. "Will you forgive me?"

Elizabeth blinked, but relaxed her stiff posture. She lifted her lips in a small smile. "Since I agree with your last statement and you have promised not to repeat such behavior, I will forgive you." She tilted her head as her fine eyes examined his features. "I was not expecting such a strong reaction."

Darcy shrugged. He gave her hand one more squeeze before letting it go. "I received a note this morning, as well. I did not read it. Now, I wish I had." His lips turned down at the corners. "I am uncertain I *will* read it, after seeing what she wrote to you. I can say with surety, however, that I will be cutting off contact with her. I will not have you spoken of in such terms, and denigrated."

"Are you certain you wish to cut off your relationship with her in such a way?"

Darcy nodded, a swift and decisive movement of his head. "I am. She has been allowed too much freedom in how she views me, as well as how she treats those around her. I will not have it. She is not permitted to treat Mrs. Darcy so infamously."

Elizabeth watched him a minute longer and then, with a sigh, conceded. "Very well. I hate to be the cause of a breach in your family, but you appear to be set on it, so I will say nothing else."

"Thank you, my love." Darcy spent the rest of the evening assiduously attending to his betrothed.

When he entered his rooms later that night, he immediately sat down and did exactly what he told Elizabeth he would do. He composed a letter to Lady Catherine expressing his displeasure and assuring her that she would not be received in any of his homes until such time as she apologized to Elizabeth. He handed it to Smith with instructions that it be sent express at first light. Then, he completed his ablutions for the night and fell instantly asleep.

~~~***~~~

On the first Monday in December, Mr. Bennet, pushed by Mr. Hill, escorted his two eldest daughters down the aisle of Longbourn's church toward the altar. He handed each of them over to their groom with a wink and a smirk, and allowed himself to be wheeled back to sit beside his wife.

Caroline Bingley watched with envy from her seat beside Louisa. On her other side was her own future husband, Lord Blackwell. Knowing she would be soon called "Lady Blackwell" alleviated some of her jealousy, for despite being tied for life to an arrogant, controlling, and unfashionable mountain of a man, she would have precedence over the new Mrs. Darcy. Still, she was not certain she would ever forgive her brother for forcing her to accept Lord Blackwell. She was equally unsure Louisa's sin of supporting Charles could ever be forgotten. She sniffed as the happy couples walked arm in arm toward the register.

"Come, Caroline." Blackwell's deep voice drew her attention to his hand, extended toward her. "We must join the rest of the crowd to congratulate your brother."

Caroline frowned and stood on her own. She pretended not to see her betrothed's smirk. She glared at him when he grasped her hand and tucked it in the crook of his elbow, patting her fingers when he was done and resting his own over them.

~~~***~~~

To Darcy's delight, his sister had been eager to visit Netherfield, get to know his betrothed, and attend his wedding. Escorted by her new governess, Mrs. Annesley, and her cousin, Colonel Fitzwilliam, she threw herself into her brother's arms the moment she stepped down from the carriage. Darcy held her close for a long moment, whispering to her his happiness at seeing her and his love for her.

Georgiana took to Elizabeth immediately. Though at first shy and reserved, she could not maintain such distance when her then soon-to-be-sister teased her and made her giggle. Within minutes, the pair were linking arms and chattering like magpies, leaving Darcy in the dust behind them. He was astonished at first, but then grinned. He decided instantly that he could not be happier at the situation.

Georgiana's arrival gave Kitty and Lydia an opportunity to speak to her directly about her experiences. None of the three would share what they spoke of – Georgiana had apparently sworn them to silence – but the behavior of the youngest of the Bennet ladies, from that day forward, was a bit more cautious, if not circumspect. The three became close, lifelong friends that day.

~~~***~~~

Hours later, Darcy and Elizabeth boarded his coach for the trip to London. As they snuggled together under a blanket, they spoke of their dreams and hopes. Darcy kissed his wife's nose. "You are your father's favorite, and I can see why. You have become my favorite, too."

With a roll of her eyes and a laugh, Elizabeth cuddled closer. "I received a letter from your cousin, Anne, today, full of congratulations on our marriage."

Darcy chuckled. "I got one, too. She was amusing in her gratitude, to be honest."

"She was." Elizabeth hugged his waist. "I would love to meet her. Perhaps we can invite her to visit? Perhaps while Mary is with us; it would do my sister a world of good to make a new friend."

"If we can get her away from her mother, we will try." Darcy kissed his wife's hair. "Thank you for being so open to making her acquaintance. After the way Lady Catherine behaved toward you, you would be justified in banning both of them from our homes."

"I could not do that." Elizabeth sat up. "She is your cousin. She is an innocent victim as much as I am."

Darcy pulled her closer. "True." He paused. "What say you we put our relatives to the side for the trip to town and pursue oth-er, more pleasant, activities?"

Elizabeth's brows rose. "Such as?"

In response, Darcy covered her lips with his. So began a long life of love.

The End

Before you go ...

If you enjoyed this book, please consider leaving a review at the store where you purchased it.

Also, consider joining my mailing list by visiting this link:
https://mailchi.mp/ee42ccbc6409/zoeburtonsig nup

~Zoe

About the Author

Zoe Burton first fell in love with Jane Austen's books in 2010, after seeing the 2005 version of Pride and Prejudice on television. While making her purchases of Miss Austen's novels, she discovered Jane Austen Fan Fiction; soon after that she found websites full of JAFF. Her life has never been the same. She began writing her own stories when she ran out of new ones to read.

Zoe lives in a 100-plus-year-old house in the snow-belt of Ohio with her Boxer, Jasper. She is a former Special Education Teacher, and has a passion for romance in general, *Pride and Prejudice* in particular, and stock car racing.

Connect with Zoe Burton

Email:
zoe@zoeburton.com

Facebook Page:
https://www.facebook.com/ZoeBurtonBooks

Burton's Babes Facebook Readers Group:
https://www.facebook.com/groups/BurtonsBabes/

Pinterest:
https://www.pinterest.com/zoeburtonauthor/

Instagram:
https://www.instagram.com/zoeburtonauthor/

Website:
https://zoeburton.com

Join my mailing list:
https://mailchi.mp/ee42ccbc6409/zoeburtonsignup

Support me at Patreon:
https://www.patreon.com/zoeburtonauthor

Me at Austen Authors:
http://austenauthors.net/zoe-burton/

More by Zoe Burton

Regency Single Titles:

I Promise To...

Lilacs & Lavender

Promises Kept

Bits of Ribbon and Lace

Decisions and Consequences

Mr. Darcy's Love

Darcy's Deal

The Essence of Love

Matches Made at Netherfield

Darcy's Perfect Present

Darcy's Surprise Betrothal

To Save Elizabeth

Darcy Overhears

Merry Christmas, Mr. Darcy!

Darcy's Secret Marriage

Darcy's Christmas Compromise

Darcy's Predicament

Darcy's Uneasy Betrothal

Darcy's Yuletide Wedding

Darcy's Unwanted Bride

Victorian Romance:

A MUCH Later Meeting

WESTERNS:

Darcy's Bodie Mine

Bundles:

Darcy's Adventures

Forced to Wed

Promises

Mr. Darcy Finds Love (available exclusively to newsletter subscribers)

The Darcy Marriage Series Books 1-3

Mr. Darcy, My Hero

Coming Together

Christmas in Meryton

The Darcy Marriage Series:

Darcy's Wife Search

Lady Catherine Impedes

Caroline's Censure

Pride & Prejudice & Racecars

Darcy's Race to Love

Georgie's Redemption

Darcy's Caution

Made in the USA
Columbia, SC
22 July 2024

39179873R00089